THE SONG OF THE
RED SIREN

ANN BARTON

Text copyright 2018 Ann Barton

Cover design by charlyn_designs

Publisher: Youngston Publishing

Printed in the United States of America

ISBN 978-0-578-74249-6

Library of Congress Cataloging-in-Publication Data has been applied for.

DEDICATION

to

**Those who GIVE and those who
RECEIVE unconditional LOVE**

TABLE OF CONTENTS

Part One

Chapter 1:   The Killing..1
Chapter 2:   The Shadow People 10
Chapter 3:   The Dream..21
Chapter 4:   The Nightmare 30
Chapter 5:   The Unbelievable 33
Chapter 6:   The Living 41
Chapter 7:   The Change 45
Chapter 8:   The Veil 49
Chapter 9:   The Friend 79

Part Two

Chapter 10: The Family..85
Chapter 11: The Unknown...93
Chapter 12: The Announcement 107
Chapter 13: The Forgiving..124
Chapter 14: The Unveiling 135
Chapter 15: The Moving 147
Chapter 16: The Graduate...161
Chapter 17: The Trouble 164
Chapter 18: The Hard Case 174
Chapter 19: The Betrayal...187
Chapter 20: The Four Words 195

CHAPTER ONE

The Killing

"*When given the healing time–we begin to forget. When the healing time has passed–do we dare to remember?*"

In the beginning, the year is 1930.

The two policemen closed their notebooks, tipped their hats, and trudged down the cold, dimly-lit hallway.

Eighteen-year-old Jenny Parsons leaned against the open apartment doorway. She endured the same questions and they listened to similar answers as last week. Yes, she'd heard the fighting and shouting in the downstairs apartment earlier. No, she wasn't aware of any stabbing. She'd left early to go to the clinic, and just returned home.

She hugged herself, buttoned her sweater against the chill, and closed the ugly brown door. Staring into the bedroom mirror, she surveyed her image. At the clinic, the doctor verified her hopes.

+++

"You're two months pregnant and weigh ninety pounds. No weight loss, or you could lose the baby," the clinic doctor cautioned.

Pregnant! Oh, that beautiful word! Johnny and I are having a baby!

The doctor completed the exam--everything was fine-- and left her to dress. She made the next monthly appointment for an afternoon, knowing Johnny would be with her.

Jenny went to rest on a bench in the hall. After hearing such thrilling news, she wanted to yell at the top of her lungs. Instead, thoughts of her growing-up years crept into her mind. This time she let herself feel the rage of despair without fear.

+++

It was a sad thing to get dumped on a tyrannical grandmother at the age of six. Worst of all wasn't the physical and mental abuse, but the absence of all caring, kindness and love. The constant criticizing and never allowed to say Grandmother, just Lady, hurt deeply.

+++

The nurse brought Jenny into the present with a tap on her shoulder.

"We're closing. Could I give you a ride? You've been sitting out here a long time."

"No, thanks, it's not far." Jenny shook herself out of her reverie and left the building, walked three blocks home, and let the cold freeze the past.

+++

I must be strong. We'll move into a nice neighborhood. I'll get a part-time job, if I have to.

Jenny chose her only nice dress: red, long-sleeved, with a plastic matching belt, red patent-leather low Cuban-heel pumps, and a black hat with curled feathers pasted on the side. She left a few dark curls poking out.

Within minutes, familiar footsteps bounced down the hall. "That will be my Johnny!"

He rushed in, five foot eleven, with black hair, blue eyes, and slender. Even at twenty, his face showed a lifetime of hard work.

"Jenny, my sweet darling." He grabbed her around the waist, and her hat fell off. "We are moving out of this dump!"

He danced her around the cold room. "My hard work paid off... Marty's moving his business to New Jersey. He wanted me to go, but with my night classes almost finished, my buddy and I can open our own car-repair shop. A lot of people in this town know my work; I can have their business!

Marty is including a bonus in my last paycheck, wants to give it to me tonight! Finally, we'll have a real home, a safe home. Dreams do come true!"

"That's wonderful, but you promised we could go to the little café tonight, Johnny! I need to talk with you about something important," Jenny pleaded.

"This will only take a few minutes. Let's stay out all *night*, go to Tufano and really celebrate! Jenny, the money is a down payment on our new home!"

Imagination by Glenn Miller played on a little radio on the counter. Johnny hugged Jenny again, and danced a few more slow steps, bodies clinging.

"Your soft creamy skin reminds me of the Snow-White porcelain dolls in Marshall Fields 'window, not to mention the sexiest body in the world." He spun her around. "Get your coat, lady. I'm going down the hall to our freezer." This was their private joke about the unheated bathroom they shared with other tenants. He winked and pulled his coat collar up around his ears.

They walked onto the street. There sat the old car. Johnny spent all his free time repairing and replacing its parts, just to keep it running. He opened her door.

"This is the first piece of junk I'm going to leave behind." He had to push the gas and clutch several times. When the engine started, he turned the headlights on.

"I looked at a 1928 Model A Ford station wagon the other day. It was made for us. I'm so happy."

"Johnny, you've worked for Marty for a year." She lifted her hands in frustration. "I've never even met your co-workers. Aren't you all friends?"

"Marty don't like no fooling around. When I told him, I wasn't moving to New Jersey, I thought he would be mad, but he stood in the office and hugged me. Said I was like a son to him." He glanced at Jenny and hoped those words would satisfy her.

Not that there was anything to be afraid of, but he *had* taken on more duties than just mechanic. His knowledge of Marty's entertainment business, especially financial, and talk of prostitution kept him from asking questions. He'd been trying to think of a reason to quit, while working overtime and saving every possible penny. He knew that he could get another job; it was just a matter of time.

As they rode silently across east Chicago, Jenny looked at the bleak and hopeless streets; a bum slept on a cold bench, dirty newspaper cluttered the alleys. She put her hand on her stomach and wished for her baby to be a boy and look like his father. *My family, our new life, will be perfect.*

"Sorry I messed up your plans tonight, Jen. I swear this will only take a minute."

"That's all right, big spender. You'll pay for it later," she said with a saucy smile. "I think you made a wrong turn. Didn't you see the Exchange Street sign?"

"No, babe, we're going across town, by the train station. Marty is taking the train to Jersey tonight. He'll probably come out and say hi. I told everyone about my beautiful wife, and he probably wants to see for himself."

Johnny stopped the car at a warehouse loading dock and stepped out. "Wait here, and leave the motor running, so you stay warm. It's freezing out here."

"Well don't take long. I know how guys are when they get together. I love you."

"Love you too. Be right back."

+++

She watched him walk into the building, head lowered, hands in his pockets.

How lucky I am. With Johnny, Jenny had discovered unconditional love, the one someone whose arms around her created the security she'd never known. *The best day of my life came after being married six months. On that morning, as with all mornings, Johnny said, "Bye, I love you."*

And terrified but hopeful, for the first time, I managed to stutter, "I love you, too."

Then, Johnny turned, ran down the hall, swooped her into his arms, and smothered her with kisses, until they were both breathless. She had never said those words to anyone else.

They had met at Robbie's party a year ago. Johnny, an orphan, had left the orphanage one day and never returned. His strength and determination changed his future, as he chose to fulfill his dreams with school and work.

Together, they created a sound foundation in love, laughter, and faith. They wanted a child. With their miserable childhoods now behind them, both believed they had love enough for many babies.

+++

Fifteen minutes passed. Jenny eased over to Johnny's seat and breathed in the manly scent of his Aqua Velva aftershave.

Trying to speed things up, she stepped out of the car, leaving it running. She tried slamming the door, but as always, the damn thing wouldn't stay shut.

Just as her fingers were starting to freeze, she saw a smiling Johnny, running down the loading dock. The headlights of the car reflected off the envelope in his hand. He was laughing, holding the envelope high in the air.

Jenny started to turn, then noticed two men coming down the loading dock.

Then each man pointed a gun at Johnny, and she screamed a warning.

Gunshots blasted the quiet night.

Johnny looked at her in surprise, then fell forward, on the ground. Automatically, she began to run toward him, to help him. Then she saw the men spring toward her.

"No! Oh, my God!" A bullet creased the sleeve of her coat.

+++

Jenny ran to the still-running car and jumped in. She backed up, hit another car in her terror, then sped off. "Oh God, help me... Faster, go faster!" she shouted at the car.

In shock, tears blinding her, she took a curve too fast and smashed into a fire hydrant. Her head snapped backward, and her vision clouded. She blinked.

They're coming to kill me!

The car, unreliable at the best of times, now shut off. She turned the key again and again, trying to force the ignition on. The engine remained silent.

She looked around but saw no one on the cold, deserted street. Were they behind her, following with guns to kill her too? She didn't know.

In anguish, she beat her fist on the steering wheel.

Stumbling out of the car, she staggered down the street, leaned over a sidewalk drain and threw up. As she stepped across the drain, the heel of her left shoe stuck in the grate. With trembling hands, she pulled her foot out of the shoe and ran down the street, carrying the other shoe.

After running two blocks, she ran over to a stairwell, and took a few rapid, cold breaths, trying to calm her fluttering heart.

She leaped into a cardboard box shelter under the stairwell. It was dark, except for a dim glow from a streetlight. Stretching out on the cardboard floor, lying as flat as possible among the pile of blankets there, she heard her pursuers.

"I know damn well that bitch came this way. That piece of shit is her car."

"Oh! Look what we have here. Come on out. Papa won't hurt you," one of them said. The other laughed.

Something fell on her: A heavy body, covering her entire body—and then a heavy hand covered her mouth. She didn't bite it, as she wanted to. They were still out there… She took shallow breaths and did not dare move.

One of the men crawled into the cardboard box. "God damn, it stinks in here." He hit the heavy body on top of Jenny. "Open your eyes, you bag of homeless filth." He hit the body again.

"Wha, wha," slurred the homeless man, covering Jenny's body. He lay dead still on top of her.

"You seen a woman around here? Or would you know one if you saw one?"

"No, no," slurred the drunk. "Ain't seen nothin'."

"Come on, come on," said the other man standing on the street. "She's getting too far ahead of us."

The man in the box hit the drunk again on the head with his fist. "One day I'm coming down here, and if dirt like you is still here, I'll kill you. Everybody will thank me."

After a few minutes, Jenny felt the homeless man lift himself off her. She took a deep breath, sat up, and gagged. She could barely make out the man's features: Dirty gray shoulder-length hair, mustache, middle-aged, and smart enough to fool Johnny's killers and save her life.

Jenny and the homeless man sat looking at each other. She held her hand to her mouth to smother a cough.

"You need to get out of here. There's a way. Don't talk, don't look back, not even a glance. Just keep moving. Can you do that?" The stranger in the dim light spoke in a strong, soft, alert tone, never taking his eyes off the shelter opening.

"Yes," Jenny said trembling. "Where am I going?
Who are you?"

"Name is Dockett." He started moving things from a corner. "Take this." He grabbed a pair of filthy, foul smelling old pants, long-sleeved shirt with holes in both sleeves, a pair of laceless high-top men's shoes and a tan wool mildewed overcoat.

"You're short on time, girlie. Put the clothes over your dress and rub your hands on the bottom of the shoes and put the dirt on your face. Good. Here's a hat I found yesterday. Put it on, it'll hide your hair. You can't stay here. They may come back this way. Hell, *I* can't stay here either.

That's a mean son of a bitch. I don't know why they want you, and I don't want to know. Little lady, what they will do to you will make you beg to die. The mob hates the likes of us. If you think they know where you live, never go back! Now, let's get going."

He put on boots, and Jenny heard his voice shaking. "I need a damn drink."

Dockett led her out into the freezing night, the wind and rain whirling around them. A dirty bum wearing a bulky torn coat, several layers of clothes and a big wool cap approached them. He grabbed Dockett's coat sleeve. "Go south. I just sent 'em north."

Close to dawn, wet, cold and hungry, Dockett took Jenny to a junkyard, where five bums huddled around a fire in a barrel. The top was partially covered to keep the rain out. He pushed her toward the group and watched her stand in the freezing rain, head lowered, water slowly surrounding her boots.

Dockett turned around and kept walking. He saw Jenny's little red shoe on top of the storm drain. He reached down, pulled the shoe out, and turned around. Standing behind him, the two brutes had returned.

"God damn son of a bitch," the tall blotched-face man said. He pulled out a knife and shoved it in Dockett's ribs. Feeling his blood pouring into the drain, Dockett held the little red high-heeled shoe in his hand.

CHAPTER TWO

The Shadow People

The next few weeks were harsh, with frost every morning and two snowfalls. Most nights, the wind never stopped, creating a hazard among the old and weak. Jenny attempted to meet the homeless folks, but they either ignored her or grunted and nodded without looking. She followed them. They didn't seem to care.

There was no one to rescue her. A cold certainty twisted her innards: she could not go home, ever. So, she stayed on the streets. This life proved difficult, awakening the hidden memories she kept pushed way deep inside her heart.

+++

She had found comfort around the age of twelve, running down the dirt road to the old pauper field in the cemetery for the poor people. Spreading her thin body over the grave, she became brave enough to cry before returning to her hell at the Lady's house.

+++

Her life without Johnny was dark, carrying his baby gave her light. On an especially cold night, they gathered around the fire barrel, not speaking. A woman, Jenny had never seen before walked up to her and pushed her shoulder.

Jenny could not tell the woman's age—somewhere between forty and eighty. Bags and a hat hid most of her dirty face and body. A burlap bag hung from her neck, a huge stuffed sack draped each shoulder, and two bags were tied to her waist.

Is this thing human? Jenny backed away and felt her heart pounding in her chest.

The stranger looked from side to side, spit, and wiped her mouth on her sleeve. "I'm Maggie. I know Dockett left you here. The homeless had a better life when Dockett was a cop. After the mob killed his wife and son, he came to us. You are one lucky lady. I don't want your life story. I don't give a damn about that. I *do* give a damn that you cost Dockett his life."

Startled, Jenny turned to face the woman who was warming her back to the fire barrel.

"I—I don't know what you mean."

The woman started humming "*Amazing Grace*". Jenny wanted to run, but her unending fear kept her motionless and silent.

After several minutes, neither woman moving, Maggie spoke. "Dockett died trying to help you. I better show you a few street habits, for now."

Jenny opened her mouth to say something, then thought better of it.

Maggie raised her voice, "Follow me, or you probably won't make it this winter. It's now or never! I sure as hell don't need the trouble. I owe Dockett, though, and I should try to pay up.

By the way, old Tom who lives near the warehouse, saw what happened to your friend. Said they loaded his body into the car trunk. He's probably at the bottom of the river now. He thought you were dead until he saw you a few days ago."

Jenny needed to cry. Her body was limp with the burden of grieving and surviving. She wanted to scream, but she remained silent. Maggie started walking down the alley.

Jenny ran and reached out. "Let me carry one of your bags." She touched the one on Maggie's side.

Without hesitation, Maggie pointed a knife at her. Jenny jumped back, startled.

"Don't you *ever* do that again! Next time, this knife goes straight through your ribs. There ain't a homeless creature without a knife. You touch our things, your life ends. We can't afford to care, and we damn well *cannot* afford to lose our stuff.

"I'm sorry," Jenny tried to whisper.

Maggie went on as though she hadn't spoken. "I have all I own with me." She touched a sack. "This is my home. My pots and pans here, that's my kitchen." She pointed to the bag on her left hip. "This is my bedroom." She spread both arms out. "Girlie, you either wear your bed or carry it in a sack. Winter is the best. You wear as much as you can, and at night you might be warm. All these clothes even make the concrete a little softer.

Summer is hell. Everything's in bags. You sit a lot. Gets to feeling like you're carrying the dead. Now come on. I'm getting mighty tired."

Jenny kept pace with Maggie for two blocks and watched as Maggie went down an alley beside an old grocery store. She stopped at a dirty window, barely off the ground. Bending down, she dug in the ground, found a long thin steel rod and put it at the corner of the window frame and gently pushed the window open. She motioned for Jenny to climb through.

Holding back a scream, Jenny did as she was bid. Climbing in, she stood in a two-stall bathroom—just two clean sinks and a dirty shower, but the space was warm.

Maggie leaned into the opening. "Don't just stand there; move outta my way." She threw bag after bag through the crawl space, then stumbled in, reached up and closed the window. A streetlight high over the tall building next door provided enough light to look around.

"Where are we? What are we doing?"

"Well, girlie, we are in the employee's bathroom of Mason's grocery store." Jenny leaned against the wall, a sudden onset of fear as the color left her face.

"Don't worry. Shit, these people don't work at night, and the security guard's drunk every Tuesday night. Tonight, is Tuesday night. So," Maggie said, winding up her explanation, "Tuesday night is bath night, and the shower works, but only cold water."

"What! I can't, I'm afraid. I don't want to go to jail," Jenny pleaded.

Maggie pointed at Jenny. "Look here and shut up. You're gonna go out in that store, take a minute to get your eyes adjusted, then get lice shampoo, two bars of soap, get your ass back here and wash."

Thoroughly cowed, Jenny walked around the store, found the items and returned to the bathroom.

"Get this straight," Maggie instructed. "Now that you're my shadow, I still want my damn privacy. Turn around, take those clothes off. Put that lice shampoo on all the hair on your body. Take my word for it.

Everywhere there's hair, there's lice. I'll do the same. Don't look at me. Don't talk to me."

Pulling and tugging at her clothes, trying to make herself invisible, Jenny prayed quietly, "Oh, God, get me through this."

Jenny finished her shower and put on the clothes that Maggie gave her. She threw the dirty ones in a heap in the corner. Then a sharp slap landed on the right side of her face.

"Pick that shit up. Put all those lice-infected clothes in this bag. They need cleaning."

Jenny started to cry. Maggie kept on as though she hadn't. "These clothes is *all* you got in this world. They will protect you. Comfort you. You can trade for food with 'em. These clothes mean life or death… You hear me?"

"Yes."

"Now, let's get out of here and get some sleep."

All the days began to run together for Jenny. Find food, keep warm, sleep, find food, walk, beg, sleep. There was never enough of anything.

Without asking questions, Jenny washed obediently every Tuesday, following instruction from Maggie. She continued the routine for the sake of it, making no decisions, just following instructions. Hurt controlled her. *Johnny is dead.*

One Tuesday night after they bathed, Maggie went out into the store. Since Jenny had been coming with Maggie, she had never seen her go into the merchandise area of the store. Maggie never took anything and instructed Jenny never to take anything except shampoo and soap.

When Maggie didn't come back, Jenny listened hard. She heard nothing. Maggie might be dead in the store, caught, or worse. She'd noticed at times that Maggie talked to an imaginary man called Charles. *Oh, God, I'm so tired.*

She leaned against the bathroom door to listen and then abruptly fell down as Maggie came bounding into the room and accidentally knocked into her. She held something in her hand.

"Let's get out of here." They took turns and climbed out the window. Maggie checked to see if everything was in order, exactly as they'd found it. She closed the window and buried the rod.

She stood and pushed Jenny on the shoulder. With a scared, angry look, she ordered, "Don't you ever come here without me. Do you understand, girlie?"

For a moment, Jenny went blank. "I won't. I promise."

Maggie pushed her again. "If you ever breathe a word about this, I will kill you. Do you hear me?" Jenny's trembling body gave her answer.

The next Tuesday after their bath, Jenny started down the alley. Maggie stopped her.

"We're going a different way," she said with a sly look. Cold and weary, Jenny turned and followed her. They walked behind a large black building with big exhaust fans. Jenny watched Maggie push aside a boarded-up back door. Another new door stood on the other side. She carefully opened the door and motioned for Jenny to follow.

Inside, Jenny could see row after row of washing machines, and steam pressers. It was a sanitary cleaning shop, the only dry-cleaning business in town. Maggie pulled her bags down and opened the tops of two washing machines. Jenny now realized that Maggie had taken detergent from the grocery store. What a bonanza for both of them!

She opened two machines and stuffed all her dirty clothes in. Maggie poured detergent in each machine. They didn't need money for the machines in a dry-cleaning shop. As the clothes washed, the humming machines made a lullaby sound. Jenny watched Maggie remove the clothes and start the steam presser. Oh, clean clothes with the scent of fresh roses; better than gold, Jenny dreamed.

There was a rush of cold air from the office door. Jenny looked at a man standing a few feet away. He approached Maggie who remained calm. Jenny took a few steps backwards, her head buzzed with panic.

"Tom, here's my begging money for tonight. Take it, don't get smart with me, remember I know 101 ways to get you killed, understand? What usually takes no more than an hour has dragged on for almost two hours, leaving me tired to the bone."

"Oh, go on with yourself. I'll need more next time." He walked back to the office.

Jenny stood and with a smile said, "Maggie, I think you're the homeless mob boss." Did I just see a hint of a smile on Maggie's face? she wondered.

During the weeks that followed, Jenny and Maggie continued with their everyday struggles. Maggie had Jenny climb into large garbage bins to scrounge for food and clothes.

"Now, see, I found something you're good at, girlie," she said, looking over her shoulder for strangers.

Jenny experienced nausea, not only with her pregnancy, but also from the stench of the dumpsters.

Maggie taught Jenny to put wet tobacco on insect bites, use vapor rub on exposed skin to prevent insect bites and take paregoric for everything from diarrhea to headaches.

Eventually, Jenny's mind surrendered pride and hope, while her body struggled for survival for her baby. Lately, Maggie told stories about shootings, rapes, and horrible deaths. Jenny witnessed some of the cruelty. She knew this was a dangerous life, especially for a baby.

+++

"Get up, get up." Maggie tugged at Jenny's coat sleeve. "Come on," she insisted, motioning to Jenny to follow her. After walking three blocks, they turned into the alley behind the Greasy Spoon Café. Jenny knew about it. The owner gave them food, sometimes. At the back door, a young guy stood with a broom in his hand, head cocked to the side, making smoke rings with the cigarette held in his tobacco-stained hands.

Maggie walked straight to him. "Here's the girl," she said, pointing at Jenny.

"Hi, I'm Tommy. I'm the janitor." He leaned closer toward Jenny. "The other day I overheard Jack, the owner, say he needed another girl to wait tables. Now if he hires you, he ain't gonna pay you nothing, but you get to eat. There're two rooms upstairs. If you work here, you can sleep there. Maybe there won't be so many break-ins because somebody's always here. Right now, it's just me, the cook, and one other girl. We share the bathroom. If you get any tips, you give 'em to Jack. He divides it up for us."

"She'll take it," Maggie grinned.

"Hey, not so fast," Tommy said. "Jack needs to see her. With luck, she might get the job."

Maggie started humming *"Amazing Grace"*, eyes closed.

Maggie and Jenny left the store. After a few minutes, wanting to be alone, Jenny walked one way, head lowered. Maggie walked the other with a little bounce to her steps, proud and satisfied.

The following afternoon, she found Jenny sleeping under the stairs of an old apartment building. She looked at the pathetic curled-up bundle, and Jenny heard her talking to the imaginary Charles, again.

"Damn, Maggie, you could scare a person to death."

"Hell," Maggie lectured, "Don't worry about me killing you. You gonna get *yourself* killed, staying here. Now get up and put this on."

"What's that?" Jenny looked at a dark green long-sleeved dress Maggie held up. "I'm not asking where you got that, but what am I going to do with it?"

"Get off the streets for one thing. Eat a meal for two things. Quit bothering me for three things."

"You want me to see about that job at the Greasy Spoon? Jack, or whatever his name is, doesn't want me around that place."

"Oh, yes he will. Look." Maggie reached into her bag and brought out a pair of black, small-heeled pumps. From her coat pocket, she pulled out a pair of silk stockings.

Maggie said, "The rest is up to you. Some of us are leaving. You ain't gonna fare so good without us to protect you. There's been some talk about street money. If the mob finds you homeless, you'll belong to them." Jenny took the clothes.

Maggie sure knew how to scare her, even now.

She felt clean after her shower and shampoo last night. Her teeth were in good shape, from using the discarded baking soda and toothbrush from the drugstore trash bin. Her naturally curly hair needed only a finger curl. After a once-over from Maggie, she put on the oversized, dirty overcoat and started walking across the street to the store.

"Don't forget," Maggie warned, "take that damn stinking coat off before you go in."

Taking a deep breath, Jenny went upstairs to Jack's office. He proved to be a no-nonsense businessman and looked straight at Jenny as she talked. He knew Maggie was a mother hen to Jenny, and Maggie had a good head on her shoulders.

"Jenny, how old are you?" He sat behind his desk with his elbows resting on top.

"I'm nineteen. Just had a birthday." At least, Jenny remembered something about that date from school records.

"My God, aren't you afraid living on the streets? You should be." He leaned back in his leather desk chair, waiting for the answers. "The point is, I need to know where and what you did before this?"

What do I say? What do I really think happened? She didn't know Jack well enough to tell the truth, or to say the unmentionable things.

"Jack, my husband died in a car accident a few months ago." The lies came spilling out easily. "We had been married almost a year. I guess my angel sent Maggie. I love Maggie, but she insists the streets are so dangerous, some of them are leaving."

"Jenny, I will speak very plainly." *Maggie had told him about Jenny's pregnancy. He could trust old Maggie to keep the bums away from the café. Okay, he told Maggie. If she cleans up, maybe I will take a chance.*

She shifted in her seat and prayed she wouldn't faint.

"Jenny, have you ever been in trouble with the law?"

"No," she answered, relieved. "I have a clean record. You can check at the police station. They don't know me."

She agreed to all the arrangements and was grateful for her earlier conversation with Tommy, who had told her what to expect. Jack wanted to question her further, decided to leave it alone.

He turned his eyes to a clock on the wall. "What the hell, you can start tomorrow."

+++

Time was not on Jenny's side. Her pregnancy began to show. Things went smoothly at the café. Everyone was nice, and Jack let Jenny keep some of her tips. She saved every penny and received a pay raise to .15 cent per hour, including free food. She saw less and less of Maggie and worked more and more at the café.

Tommy never did collect whatever he thought Jenny owned him. Jack caught him dipping into the cash register, fired him and ordered him never to come into the café again.

Two months passed, and Jenny had a little nest egg saved. She and Maggie began seeing each other again, just walking, not talking, no need to. They understood the feelings of hurt inside each other.

+++

In the middle of the night a freezing snow with endless wind hit the town.

"Worst in history," Jack said, the next morning.

Jenny knew homeless people took to warming shelters from such a storm. She wanted to check on Maggie, anyway. She had some news, and Maggie would be just the person to hear it. As she walked down the street, she pulled her new coat a little tighter and looked around. What a mess! Everyone must be at the church mission shelter.

As she got closer to Maggie's card house, she saw several people standing around, looking at something. Moving closer for a better look, she gasped in shock.

Maggie's heavily-clothed body lay still and lifeless on the ground.

Jenny was stunned and speechless.

An ambulance arrived.

Jim, one of the friendlier homeless men, walked over to Jenny. "You know Maggie, she could never put a roof on right. She used the cheap stuff. You gotta use the Sears-Roebuck cardboard from the warehouse dumpster. It's the best kind. Looks like hers just caved in on top of her, with all that snow, and all."

The ambulance crew removed Maggie's body, and the little group around her dispersed. Jenny sat on the pile of clothes in the corner of the lean-to cardboard home. Beneath the clothes, she found a little faded photograph of a young woman, a handsome man, and a small child. Jenny turned the picture over and read the shaky handwriting on back: Maggie, Charles, and Charles Jr.

She bent over the photograph and wept.

CHAPTER THREE

The Dream

Jenny concentrated on her work and on preparations for her baby's birth. She still suffered nightmares and heartbreaking moments, remembering Johnny dying, without her being able to give him a final farewell.

Her life of fear and survival led to the brink of insanity. She carried a heavy load at work, requesting double shifts whenever possible. *I'll take the good days and embrace them and take the bad ones and accept them. I'll just keep moving forward.*

On July 10,1931, at 3 A.M., she gave birth to a healthy seven-pound, two-ounce baby boy. After the birth, the nurses at the welfare clinic talked to her about adoption.

"No. This baby helps me know love and worth. I'll be thankful for every minute with him." She closed her eyes and whispered, "I will. I will."

She completed the birth certificate: father- unknown, mother, Jenny Timmons, and baby's name, Jeremiah Elijah Thomas. It was a strong name, to carry a strong boy into manhood. Though the birth was uneventful, her promises to the baby entered her dreams, leaving her exhausted each day.

+++

Jenny always felt a flutter in her heart when Jeremiah jumped into her arms. The little boy, who stirred her heart when he called her "Mommy," gave her the strength and courage to face life's difficulties and joys. She worked two shifts a day and saved as much as she could.

The cheap apartment Jenny had rented before the birth was located on a narrow, trash-ridden street, which caused her unreasonable guilt. The employees at the café helped with the baby. Jack often let the "little man" sleep in his office. After nearly two years of living with deep despair, after the baby's birth, Jenny became obsessed with finding a way out.

She had grown enough to understand Johnny's death was intentional. He knew something important about Marty. He had mentioned something about China several times to her. She assured herself they knew about her, but *not* about a baby. Thank God, she hadn't told Johnny that she was pregnant. She began casually inquiring about Marty. The answer made the decision she needed. He was the crime boss of East Chicago, a very tough piece of work.

+++

Jeremiah always wiggled, squirmed and babbled with bursts of giggles. He could not stay still. After repeating Jeremiah too many times, Jenny decided to use his initials J.E.T for his nickname. She noticed "Jet" responded to that name with a mischievous grin.

+++

Jack gave her the address of a little apartment in Newark, New Jersey. "I bought it for something that didn't happen. Nothing fancy, but sidewalks with trees, and the brick apartment has been well maintained. It's upstairs, but in a nice neighborhood and furnished. We'll talk about rent later. You'll do me a favor, keeping the place clean."

There wasn't much she could say to that; so, she agreed. Trusting her gut, and wanting desperately to get away from Chicago, Jenny decided to move into the upstairs apartment on Cornerstone Street in Newark. She packed and checked the Greyhound bus schedules. The apartment would be cleaned and ready in two weeks. She owned church mission give—a—ways, really very little to move, just clothes and toys for Jet.

Two-year-old Jet had black hair and blue eyes. He was the mirror image of his father. She loved playing his make-believe games, and found herself wishing for dreams lost.

For now, I want to treasure the gift of life again, this time with my son. This is my moment of joy and hope.

+++

They moved the first week in May. The weather sent a warm breeze throughout the rooms of her new home, carrying the sweet scent of the roses below the window.

The furnished apartment was clean and simple. While unpacking a box of toys, she found a set of wind chimes, a Christmas present from Johnny.

Oh my. Holding back tears, she let long-forgotten emotions rise to the surface: tenderness for her friend and lover. I had a life and a family.

"Made 'em myself," he'd said, presenting them to her with the smile that left her breathless.

The chimes consisted of circular bands of hickory, looking like embroidery hoops. Dangling down on different lengths of string were glued-on pieces of broken glass, which made fairy-like music as they brushed against one another.

The sound reached something inside Jenny that had been dormant for a long time. She hung them out the window, attached to a small tree branch, and enjoyed the moment.

She removed Jet from his make-believe cardboard train to go for a walk, which with Jet, was more like a run.

Two blocks from their apartment, a girl in a white uniform who looked about Jenny's age pointed at Jet as Jenny brought him down the street.

"He's the handsomest little boy I've ever seen," she said. "Is he yours?"

"Yes." Jenny grabbed Jet's hand and pulled him close.

"Hi. My name is Ruth Stillman. I live upstairs. Do you live near here?"

"Are you a nurse?" Jenny asked, noticing the crisp white uniform.

"Yes, I work nights at the Grady Hospital Clinic.

"I'm Jenny Timmons and this is Jet. We live on Cornerstone Street."

"Do you go to the park down the street?" Ruth asked.

"Actually, I'm looking for a job that will let me work and care for Jet. We just moved here."

"What kind of training do you have?"

"Training?"

"Yes. Medical? Secretarial school? You know?"

"Well, I cared for my grandmother. I fed her, bathed her and changed the bed."

"Let me check at the hospital. There's a nurse aide course beginning soon. I'll get the details and schedules for you. How about if I come over tomorrow? We can talk about the training and maybe take a walk in the park."

Jet pulled on Jenny's hand. "Okay. I live at 309 Cornerstone Street, apartment C."

Her face beaming, Ruth said, "Give me until three o'clock. I sleep until then, especially after a twelve-hour shift. Then I'll come over. Jet will love the park!"

Back in their cozy apartment, Jenny sobbed like a child. *I must stop being so afraid and suspicious. It's time I got on with my life.*

The next afternoon Ruth came to visit. Jet wasn't feeling well. "Can I help?"

"No, but I need to stay home. Could we visit here?"

"Sure." Ruth stood in the doorway.

Jenny tucked a blanket around Jet. "Come in. It's not great, but we like it."

"Oh Jenny, it's *darling*. I love the colors, especially the pale-yellow kitchen walls."

"Thanks. The wicker table and two upright chests came with the apartment. The coffee table and rocking chair were left on the street for pick up, so I did. And the toys that are everywhere, they came with us." She pointed at Jet.

"You have a window overlooking the street. I have a back apartment, so I only get to look at a parking lot," Ruth said.

"That's my favorite spot." Jenny raised the window to allow a gentle breeze to blow the lace curtains. Jet lay in his hammock bed looking at a picture book.

"He sure is handsome. I say 'handsome' because somehow 'cute' just doesn't seem to fit," Ruth said.

"Thanks, say it as often as you like. I happen to agree."

"He must look like his father. I can't see your features that much in his face."

Jenny responded quickly, "Oh, he's his father's image, but has my stubbornness."

Ruth blew out a long breath. "Jenny, I'd like for us to be friends. I have a feeling you could use a friend, same as me. I have no close friends here. You know I work at Grady General on the night shift. I'm not married. You sure you want to hear this mess?"

Jenny replied, "You might as well. I'm listening."

"The trouble is," Ruth explained, "I dislike the men I know, and I enjoy the women I know. Keeps me awake at night; all the what-ifs. Please don't judge me, but I prefer my present life, with no boyfriends."

Leaning forward in her chair, Jenny reached over and patted Ruth's shoulder.

"Thank you for your fairness," Ruth said. "Now, what about you?"

Jenny said nothing.

"Oh, Jenny, I'm sorry, God, let's talk about something else."

Jenny's hands trembled. She walked to the window, thinking desperately. *She needed to tell someone... had needed to for so long. God, please let this be okay. I really need a friend.*

She took a deep breath. "We moved here from Chicago, just Jet and me. Jet's father is... dead. This may be... difficult. You must never repeat what I'm going to tell you." Ruth gripped the arms of the chair. "We had to run and hide. It's so hard to explain... sometimes I'm still confused."

Ruth wanted to give Jenny a hug; instead, she sat and waited.

Jenny continued, "Johnny and I married, moved into an apartment. He got a job... the pay was good... Johnny was happy... We saved for our first home. We thought about the future. He wanted to quit his job, and was about to graduate from mechanic school… he wanted to start his own shop."

"What did Johnny do?"

Jenny shook her head, looked at the ceiling. "He was the mechanic for the company cars and kept all their records."

"Wow. That sounds important."

"I guess. They wanted him to move with them to their new office."

"Something wrong?" Ruth noticed Jenny's restlessness.

"Memories," Jenny said, her eyes closed.

"How did Johnny die?"

Jenny stared at her palms and bit down on her trembling bottom lip. "They shot him… when he went to pick up his last paycheck… I saw him fall but I didn't know if he was actually dead when I ran… to save my life and Jet's. I don't know who's to blame. We were in love and *so* naïve. I think he knew more about his company than he should have… it was too dangerous, so they got rid of him… and now all I have are my memories of that one year with him. And I have Jet, for a lifetime."

+++

The next morning, in the grim light of first dawn, Jenny hurried Jet to the movie theater, where she acquired a part-time job at the ticket counter and cleaning seats between shows. Jet was no trouble; he was just noisy and demanded her attention to play. *I need money and a safe place for Jet while I work,* she decided.

She called Ruth on Wednesday, and they planned a trip to the park the next day. Jenny made the decision to take the aide course at the hospital. To her surprise, she thought about asking Ruth to keep Jet for the two evening classes, on Ruth's days off.

Ruth arrived at Jenny's apartment at four o'clock the next afternoon, and greeted Jet.

Jenny wore a red sundress and sandals. "Jenny, I swear, you could look great in anything, even rags. I've always had the fit-here, doesn't-fit-there issue." Ruth moved her hands from her shoulders to her hips.

Jenny sighed. "When you have a Jet to run after, there's little time left to eat."

"Red looks good on you."

"Thanks. Red makes me feel strong."

"Let's get going. Jet just ran over my foot again," Ruth joked.

The three left the building, laughing and talking.

The park was a block away, and Jenny was delighted with the sumptuous playground, that had swings, slides, even a merry-go-round, surrounded by a fence, and with benches available for moms and dads. There were other people around, but it wasn't crowded. Jet ran to the swings. Ruth ran after him.

"I'll get ice cream from the vendor; can you keep up with him?"

"I'll try, get me a strawberry cone, will you?" Ruth shouted.

Jenny got the cones and walked to the swings, breathing in the smell of fresh-cut grass and sawdust. Ruth was pushing Jet high, and he was squealing with joy.

"How lucky I am," Jenny told herself. Ruth and Jenny had already shared memories, but Jenny remained cautious of telling everything, though she knew she needed a trusting friend.

+++

As Jenny sat on the playground bench, she used the time to settle the past events in her head. Although the 1920's were a period of optimism and prosperity for some Americans, many had invested in the stock market. By 1930, countries began to fall into the Depression, including the United States.

At sixteen years of age, she managed to share a room with four girls in a boarding house. She enjoyed her independence, no matter the hardships. Most of their earnings went to the landlord. The girls became her first friends. They told her she was a woman; her monthly proved it. She could have babies.

Then in 1930, Chicago and the country were forced to face the dark side of the irresponsible and lawless economy.

Food riots broke out. Al Capone opened a soup kitchen in November 1930, creating a loyal following among jobless men.

Some of the girls went into entertainment with the mob, as cocktail servers and prostitutes. One of the girls, Lucille, eventually committed suicide.

Johnny met Jenny; Jenny met the love of her life.

+++

After three hours, it took a lot of persuasion to get Jet to head home. They walked slowly, knowing they had become some kind of strange little family.

As they approached Jenny's building, she said, "Come on up and have a glass of tea. I have a great big favor to ask."

"Uh, oh," Ruth said. "What have I gotten myself into?" They went inside. Jenny reached for the tea bags on the kitchen counter.

Then the door burst open.

The three-person family would never exist again.

CHAPTER FOUR

The Nightmare

Two men grabbed Jenny's arms. Jenny clenched her fists and screamed, "Take your son and get out of here!"

With no time to think, Ruth grabbed Jet into her arms and ran into the street.

Then she heard a loud noise, and Ruth saw Jenny's face, that beautiful face, surrounded by red, break the glass window. She knew Jet heard the noise. Ruth held him close and covered his eyes with her hand. She began to run, holding onto Jet and praying not to stumble.

She saw a telephone booth, ran inside and dialed the operator, told her what she could, begged for help, then slid down inside and hugged a crying Jet.

+++

Jenny tore loose and ran to the window. Strong hands pounded the back of her head.

My face is on fire. "Don't kill me," she begged as the pieces of glass cut into every inch of her skin.

"So, you want to look out the window? How's that?" a huge man with a protruding forehead said. "It took us a while, but a bitch is a bitch. Before old homeless Tom died, he told us word was, you moved to Jersey. The bus schedule took care of the rest.

Marty don't like witnesses, and your name was in one of Marty's books. Your husband borrowed money, then decided to just... run away. Well, that's not how things work with Marty."

He grabbed her hair, pulling her across the room, pushed away the wicker chairs and threw her onto the kitchen table. She struggled to open her eyes, but the blood kept them shut. She tried to scream, but no sound came out. A rough hand tightened around her throat, and she felt like she was being smothered. She screamed on the inside. *If the pain gets bad enough, I will pass out.* She remained conscious.

The cursing big brute climbed on top of her; probing, panting, and pumping with all his strength. He let out a loud grunt of satisfaction.

She felt the burning tearing of flesh as he pulled himself out and violated her with the cold steel knife up to the handle.

"Let's finish the damn job," the other man ordered. I can't fuck that whore after your mess. Marty wants her dead and unrecognizable."

The beating began.

A police siren sounded down the street. Both men were out of breath.

Jenny's mind floated away from her suffering body to look down on her. She did not feel the slashing of her face and body, or the knife plunging deep into her back.

As the door opened downstairs, the assailants fled down the back stairway, leaving a trail of bloody shoe prints.

+++

Two uniformed policemen entered the quiet apartment building as instructed by the unidentified caller. With guns drawn, they entered apartment C.

They observed the crime scene: walls, table, and chairs, all covered with blood. The younger cop slipped on the blood-puddled floor as he bent down to check the body. "No pulse." He stood, looking pale and sick.

The older cop knelt and turned Jenny's body over. The young policeman looked again, leaned over and vomited.

"Damn," the veteran cop said, "I've been on the force fifteen years, and I never seen such violence. What the hell did this woman get into?"

"Harry, Harry!" shouted the young cop. "Look at her left hand!"

"What the hell? How in the hell?" Harry watched as two bloody fingers ever so slightly moved.

"Call for an ambulance. Tell 'em to hurry. She's alive. My God, if she lives—" he said softly.

CHAPTER FIVE

The Unbelievable

Ruth's entire body wanted to run, scream, cry. Instead, she walked down the street to her apartment, trying not to attract attention while keeping Jet calm.

Her shaking hands and trembling body made it difficult getting the key in the door.

Jet kept whimpering, "I want Mommy."

Ruth was holding him when she heard the sirens go by her apartment. She closed her eyes and mumbled, "God, please don't let it be too late'"

+++

Ruth paced back and forth. Jet was eating his favorite peanut butter and jelly sandwich. She held back tears somehow, trying to think clearly. *I'm supposed to work tonight.* She had no choice.

She called the supervisor at the volunteer care center at the hospital.

"Martha, this is Ruth Stillman. Do you have an opening for a two—year-old tonight?" she asked, keeping her fingers crossed. "My sister has cancer, and I have my two-year-old nephew with me."

Martha assured her she had space, and Ruth could drop him off while she worked. *Thank God, I have a safe place for Jet tonight. I'll check on Jenny while I'm on duty. I hope the ambulance made it in time.*

At ten o'clock, Ruth called a cab to take her and a tearful Jet to Grady Hospital.

Upon arrival, she hurried to the children's care center.

Martha met Ruth and exclaimed, "Oh, what a beautiful little boy. Ruth, I'm sorry to hear about your sister."

"Thanks, Martha. I appreciate your help on such short notice."

Jet's eyelids blinking shut signaled he was getting sleepy, and Ruth was grateful for that.

Martha prepared a small cot for Jet with a teddy bear on the pillow. Ruth tucked him in and kissed him on the cheek, just as Jet fell asleep.

After she left Jet, she walked, almost ran, to the ER. She needed to know if Jenny was alive.

"Yes," the triage nurse said, "Jane Doe was brought in, barely alive. She's in surgery."

Ruth had a never-ending amount of work on her shift. She had three admissions to process but still checked on Jet several times. He had been sleeping fitfully, calling for his mommy.

Without taking a break, at six a.m., she hastened to Jenny's post-op room.

Jenny's entire head and face were covered in bandages. One arm was in a cast. A blood transfusion as well as other fluids were running intravenously. A chest tube was draining into a suction bottle. Ruth knew whatever the two men did, their intension was murder.

She went to the nursery once more to check on Jet. This time, he slept.

"Could you give me a few hours of sleep?" She asked Martha, hopefully. Ruth was having trouble breathing, her nerves heightened.

"I'll call you if he wakes up, I promise. Now you go home and try to rest," Martha said softly.

Ruth hailed a taxi. She wouldn't walk that street alone, not yet. She went inside, showered, and collapsed on the sofa. Frightening images of Jenny's face at the window and the evil monsters behind her, froze in her dreams.

After two hours of sleep, she woke with a splitting headache. She ate a few bites of toast, drank some strong coffee and dressed in a clean uniform, still confused and frightened.

What in the world happened? I know those men tried to kill Jenny. What should I do? God, help me, please.

Ruth's mind raced while her body slowed down. She remembered the horrified look on Jenny's face. She did not want those men to know she had a son. Jenny had told her no paperwork was involved with the apartment move, just a handshake. If Jenny remained in the hospital, a complete investigation would begin as soon as the hospital staff would allow. Jenny would never be safe in the hospital or even in this town.

+++

Ruth opened her apartment door to leave for the hospital and saw Ralph, the man down the hall. He smiled, snapped on his little black dog's leash and opened the front door. He always walked all the way to the hospital.

I've never been afraid to walk to the hospital until today. Those men could be anywhere. I feel safe, knowing someone would be on the sidewalk, within calling distance.

Ruth went straight to the children's care center. Jet was curled up asleep, hugging the teddy bear.

She waved at Martha, "I'm going for coffee. Back in a few minutes."

She smiled at the staff working in the critical care unit and went directly to Jenny's room, opened the door and quietly entered.

Everything seemed the same. Jenny was unconscious, with a ventilator providing regulated breaths.

As Ruth stepped into the hallway, she noticed a policeman at the desk, talking to the nurses. Frightened, but determined to get some answers, she quickly formed a plan.

Ruth walked to the other side of the nurses' station, and out of their view, she pulled Jenny's chart.

The sheet listed no personal information. *Thank God.* She read the surgeon's report: Complete hysterectomy performed, partial removal left lung due to stab wound, right kidney removed, multiple fractures to facial area, unable to repair facial lacerations, tissue destruction, bone displacement, fractured right arm. Patient placed in medical coma. Condition: critical. Prognosis: poor.

Ruth's mind zigzagged through a dozen thoughts. *I need to work and keep an eye on Jenny without anyone noticing. I'll care for Jet as his Aunt Ruth and avoid questions about the two of us. I must remain strong and in control. A friend sticks close when she's needed, and Jenny is my friend. The police know nothing about Jet or me. The attackers think Jenny is dead. Oh, God, I hope they think she's dead.*

+++

Months passed.

Jenny had multiple surgeries, with many complications. Infection proved to be her worst enemy. With the ventilator removed, she breathed on her own now.

She remained at Grady Hospital, though needing less critical nursing care.

Ruth knew that the treatment team would soon meet and suggest a plan of continuing care outside of Grady. Jenny was indigent. The hospital received no reimbursement for her care. The administration would be anxious to transfer her.

Also, the possibility of a police investigation into Jenny's broken world struck terror into Ruth. Why did those men need Jenny dead? Who was to blame for almost killing her?

While dealing with the confusion of her life, Ruth decided to make Jet's life less complicated. He had difficulty pronouncing certain words. He could not easily be understood, especially calling Ruth his new friend.

"Jet", Ruth said. "I love you very much. From now on, just call me Aunt Ruth."

"Is that what Mommy calls you?" he asked.

"Yes, she told me to tell you. So, how about it, partner?"

"Okay," he replied, and his smile gave her the strength and the determination to keep him safe.

+++

At three o'clock in the morning, Ruth rushed in to see Jenny before finishing her shift.

At the nurses' station, she was shocked to read: Patient awake, refuses communication, wounds healing, will continue rehabilitation therapies, psychiatric consult.

Ruth had a thought that made her head hurt, but she'd already made the decision: *This way out.* From experience, she knew it was routine for the psychiatrist to wait until at least two weeks after a consult order, especially if heavy medical issues were involved.

+++

Immediately, she requested a week off and borrowed a friend's car. She could not rent one, as she'd never bothered to get a driver's license. She could drive, though.

Ruth picked up Jet at the employee child-care center. At the apartment, she packed as little as possible, and then maneuvered the four hours to Apalachin, New York with Jet. She had visited the small town once with a friend to see a patient at the public mental health hospital and recalled the staff's caring attitude. The hospital accepted mentally ill patients with medical issues, and the distance would not present any transfer problems.

After getting a room at the Continental Hotel, she allowed Jet some playtime and searched the real-estate ads in the local newspaper. She needed an apartment within walking distance of the Johnston Mental Health Hospital.

"You're in luck," the realtor said. "A furnished one-bedroom studio apartment will be available in about two weeks." Ruth put down a deposit, signed the lease, and drove home, feeling tired and anxious. *At least, the decision is behind me.* The pressure had taken its toll on her.

Her life revolved around Jet's safety, and her love for him and his mother. She described Jenny to Jet and tried to explain that Mommy would get well soon and come home.

The next week's routine was packing, working, and thinking of new games for Jet. Finally, it was time.

Ruth dressed in uniform to complete her plans. She took Jet to the day center and made her way to the nursing station on Jenny's floor.

No one saw Ruth as she wrote carefully on the doctor's order form on Jenny's chart: Transfer patient to Johnston Mental Health Hospital, Apalachin, New York, by ambulance when stable. She signed the consulting psychiatrist's name.

Jenny needs to be out of this town; yet still watched closely by hospital staff, Ruth decided.

Using the excuse of her sick sister, Ruth took a month's leave of absence from her job. She called Johnston Hospital admissions, identified herself as the transferring nurse from Grady Hospital and stated that medical records would accompany the patient.

She then talked to Pete, an older man at the hospital loading dock, who also worked part-time for the North American Moving Company, and for a fee, he moved Ruth's belongings to the new apartment at Apalachin.

While they waited to complete the remainder of the plan, Ruth and Jet camped out at their present apartment, sleeping on blankets, and using wooden crates for a table.

+++

On her second night back at work, Ruth took a quick break and went directly to the nursing station in charge of Jenny's care. She noticed Jenny's chart was not on the chart rack. She entered her room; the bed was empty.

Trying to stay calm, Ruth approached Kathy, the charge nurse. "Catch me up on the Jane Doe patient."

"She was transferred to Johnston Mental Hospital yesterday." Kathy leaned over and whispered, "I'm glad she's gone. Whatever they did to her made us a little afraid up here."

"Did the police ever find out what happened?" Ruth asked.

"They don't have a clue. They think it's another prostitute/John deal gone wrong. It's a shame. Another cold case, was the message I got."

"Too bad."

"Yeah... Ruth, what did you need?"

"Oh, I came to see if you had an extra IV set."

"Sure, grab one out of the supply closet. How's your sister doing?"

"About the same, thanks for asking."

Once again, Ruth took action as if being guided. It was three in the morning, and the halls of the old hospital were quiet and dim. Using the back stairs, she made her way to the medical records department, stayed out of sight, and waited till the desk clerk left on her break.

Dear God what am I doing? I barely know Jenny. I could lose my license, go to jail, and Jenny and Jet would be lost forever.

"Stop." She said it out loud, trying to get rid of the conflicting thoughts. "Jenny is my friend." Then Ruth searched the discharge file cabinet for Jenny's chart. The psychiatrist's assistant assessed Jenny and did not question the transfer order. Her notes read, "Unable to communicate. Patient despondent. Transfer as ordered."

Maintaining her made-up relative problem, Ruth had a lengthy discussion with her supervisor, turned in her resignation, and promised to return if her sister's condition improved.

Ruth and Jet moved into the new apartment on Broad Street in Apalachin, and Ruth began using her savings to pay the bills.

CHAPTER SIX

The Living

Jenny's transfer to the Johnston Mental Health Hospital increased the pain in her body, and medication to relieve the pain pushed her into the deep, dark, painful jungle in her mind.

+++

The next three months were filled with anguish, as the staff probed and prodded her, looking for ways to restructure her shattered body.

Whenever she tried to move, something tight wrapped around her. Too often, they gave her an injection and she drifted back into darkness.

+++

"Miss. Miss. Can you hear me?"

She strained to open her eyes and saw what she assumed was a doctor in a white coat, with a stethoscope around his neck. She tried to read his name tag.

"Where am I?" Jenny whispered.

The doctor said calmly, "I am Dr. Buchanan. You are a patient at Johnston Mental Health Hospital in Apalachin, New York. Whenever we let you out of the restraints, you hit the staff and try to get out of bed."

"Restraints? Please tell me where I am and how did I get here?" Jenny struggled to remain calm. She could only whisper. Her entire face hurt when she tried to speak.

Dr. Buchanan pulled his chair close to the bed.

He looked over at Jenny's bandaged head. Only her eyes, nose and mouth were unwrapped.

"You were a patient at Grady Hospital. They treated you until you stabilized. When you became conscious, you tried to remove your bandages and refused treatment. Your doctors decided to transfer you here for a complete psychiatric evaluation."

Jenny blinked her eyes. "How long have I been here?" she asked, trying to control her agitation.

Dr. Buchanan replied, "Three months. You've been heavily medicated for your own protection." He rose, pushed back his chair, and patted Jenny's shoulder. "I'll be back in the morning. Get some rest. Your body has defied all odds so far, but you're not ready for discharge, yet."

Jenny could not comprehend what the doctor had said. She hunched her shoulder to touch her face, which hadn't stopped hurting. All she felt was a big bulky bandage. *If I take this bandage off, maybe my headache will go away.*

As she attempted to get out of her restraints, a nurse came in.

"Oh, no, you don't, not on my shift!" She quickly pushed Jenny's shoulders down on the pillow, gave the straitjacket strap a pull, found the syringe in her pocket and gave her a shot in the hip. "Now sleep and stay out of trouble."

Jenny closed her eyes in total confusion. *What have I done?*

+++

After Jenny's admission, Ruth visited the mental hospital many times and joined a hospital volunteer group to help in the facility. She knew hospitals well enough to know they would never turn down a volunteer. She chose two hours in the afternoon, allowing Jet playtime in the hospital's children activity area.

After six weeks of volunteer orientation, Ruth rolled the flower cart to patient rooms for delivery of the beautiful arrangements.

Ruth ordered flowers, signed from "A Friend". The following day on her shift, she noted their arrival at the hospital and placed them on her cart.

As she approached the nursing station, the charge nurse looked up from her desk.

"Who's getting flowers?" she asked. "They're beautiful."

Ruth showed her the card.

"Oh," the nurse said. "Jane Doe can't have flowers or visitors, until she tells us what happened. Too bad, she just might enjoy these." The nurse leaned over to smell the roses.

"Okay," Ruth said, "I'll leave the flowers at the desk." She noted that the nurse seemed talkative. Then Ruth said casually, "My last home-care patient had mental problems. I was allowed to sit in on her therapy sessions."

"How did it turn out?" the nurse asked.

"Well, it took a while, but she's now a happily married woman starting a new life," Ruth said, making it up as she went on. "During your shift, ask Jane Doe if she'd like to talk with someone who wants to listen. You can tell her my name is Ruth."

"Sure," said the charge nurse while she filled med cups, "but I need to tell you something. Some of her bandages were removed. She has extensive damage to her face. Would this be a problem?"

"No. I'm an RN, but with child-care problems. I'm volunteering on my own."

The nurse looked over her shoulder and whispered, "Maybe you could get some answers for us. Grady Hospital had nothing except her medical and surgical notes." While walking away, pushing the med cart, she told Ruth, "Keep all information confidential except to the staff. If your visits upset her, you need to let us know."

Two weeks later, Ruth went to Jenny's floor when she knew the same charge nurse would be on duty. "Hi," Ruth said to the nurse, "remember me?"

"Sure," the nurse answered. "Oh, by the way, I talked with the patient we discussed last time, Jane Doe in 624, and believe it or not, she said yes, or at least, I *think* she said yes."

Ruth started toward the room and could barely hold back the tears. No matter what, she was determined to let Jenny know Jet was okay.

She pushed the door open and stood at the foot of her friend's bed. Sick patients were no strangers to Ruth. This time, though, she was already attached to this patient by love. She slowly approached the bed and touched Jenny's hand.

"Jenny," she whispered, "it's me, Ruth. Don't try to talk." Ruth noticed a small movement in the bandaged face as Jenny reached out her hand. "Don't talk," Ruth repeated. "I can't stay long. Jenny, please listen. No one here knows that I know you. I'm here as a volunteer. This way they can't connect us."

Jenny was struggling to speak, and Ruth recognized only one word. "*Jet.*"

CHAPTER SEVEN

The Change

Jenny endured months of facial skin grafts. She travelled by ambulance to the outpatient plastic surgery center for each procedure. A cumbersome, weighty bandage supported the sutured skin. Only her eyes, nose, and mouth were left exposed. Her internal wounds were healing without complications.

Ruth visited as often as she could, with news about Jet. During each visit, Jenny insisted Ruth help her walk around the room and talk about Jet. She gave specific instructions about him.

"Tell Jet his mother is on a long trip and loves him very much. Maybe one day, I will see him from a distance," Jenny said.

Outside Jenny's room, Ruth struggled with Jenny's words. She didn't quite comprehend the meaning.

On the morning of December 5th, a nurse and social worker entered Jenny's room.

"You're being discharged tomorrow, after almost a year of treatment and therapy. Your doctors have deemed you competent to care for yourself. We need to contact your family for discharge plans." The social worker waited for a response. "Did you understand what I said?" she asked.

Jenny, still posing as a Jane Doe, remained silent.

The social worker put papers on the bedside table. "I need you to complete the paperwork. This folder contains your follow-up appointments. Please leave a forwarding address and a phone number. Any questions?"

"No."

"I will write on your chart that you are arranging your care after discharge."

+++

Jenny hastened to her bathroom and locked the door. The time had come to see her body. She had been receiving bed baths and refused to look into the bathroom mirror. *Well, I need to see what everyone else saw. I'm on my own. I'm ready to get out of here.*

Trembling, she let her gown drop to the floor. One look in the mirror caused such nausea, she turned and threw up in the toilet. After rinsing her mouth, she braced herself for another nightmare.

Railroad-track suture lines crisscrossed her 100-lb. body. Slopes of missing skin had left red, irregular patches on her thighs, and stomach. She twisted her head to look at her back and cried until she was exhausted.

She crawled into bed, dreading the future. *Until I can understand Johnny's death, I have to keep my precious son a secret.* She closed her eyes with a prayer: *God, take care of Jet and Ruth.*

+++

Ruth came to visit that afternoon with a container of red roses, but Jenny remained quiet.

After a few moments, Ruth commented, "I brought you a pair of pants and a shirt for your physical therapy. They won't look great, but anything beats that hospital gown. There's some cash in each pocket, in case you want to bribe your therapist into an easy workout. I know how patients manage the staff. Anything I need to know about?"

Jenny looked up at her friend. "They gave me some medicine. I think I'm just sleepy."

"Well, I'm out of here. Oh, Jet has two new friends in play care. One's having a birthday party at his house. I thought it would be nice for him to go."

"Yes. Oh yes," Jenny mouthed.

"I bought a present for him to take," Ruth continued. "He picked it out himself. By the way, you and I should plan a birthday party for Jet with a clown, balloons and ice cream. You'll need to set the date," Ruth chattered on, not noticing the tear in Jenny's eye.

She couldn't ask Ruth for more than she was already doing. She had to handle this on her own.

The following day, the nurse placed Jenny in a wheelchair and rolled her to the hospital entrance to release her.

A taxi pulled up to the curb. "You're going home in a taxi?" the nurse questioned.

"Yes. Thanks, I'll be fine. They have everything waiting for me." Jenny tried to sound convincing.

The nurse looked around. "I don't know about this. Well, only if you promise to go see the doctor at the clinic in two weeks."

"I promise." Jenny waved good-bye and the taxi pulled into the oncoming traffic.

"Where to, lady?" the driver asked.

"The Queen of Angels Catholic Church Women's Mission Shelter," Jenny said, almost apologizing.

"Hey, just a minute. You got money for this ride? If you don't, you get out here."

"I have the money," she said.

The taxi driver looked in the rear-view mirror. "Show me some cash."

Jenny reached into her pants pocket and showed him a five-dollar bill. *Bless Ruth again. Oh, Ruth, I need you so much. My son needs you more.*

CHAPTER EIGHT

The Veil

At nine o'clock on a cold December morning, Jenny entered the Women's Mission Shelter. She walked slowly to a desk in a corner of the small lobby.

A short, plump Negro woman stood up, both hands on her hips. "If you came looking for a home, let me just set you straight. You can only stay for three months. This is a *temporary* shelter."

"I understand," Jenny answered.

"How old are you?" the woman asked, walking from behind her desk.

"I'm twenty-four years old."

"Show me some identification."

"I'm sorry. My things were lost. I was in an accident."

"Is that why you have bandages on your face? We don't need no trouble here."

"I can take these bandages off, but my face hurts without them."

The woman handed her a pile of paper. "Fill out these forms and bring them back to me. Can you read and write?"

"Yes."

"Sit over there." She pointed to the other side of the room. "Use the pen on the desk, and make sure you leave it there when you're finished."

Sitting at the desk, Jenny looked through the papers, not at them. She touched the wet bandages around her eyes. She had no idea how to answer the questions.

"Aren't you done yet?" shouted the woman from across the room.

Jenny jumped and swallowed hard to keep from screaming.

She felt her hurting, bulky face with her hand. "No, I'm—I'm a little tired." She looked at the forms. Everything she wrote on them would be a lie. It would have to be, if she was to have *any* chance of safety in this new life.

She listed her name as Jenny I. Stone, which she felt suited her feelings; they felt cold and hard. There would be no prince coming to rescue her.

She completed the pages, lying with every answer, and took them to the woman at the desk.

The woman glanced at the forms while Jenny stood, shifting from one foot to the other, trying to remain upright.

"I don't want to hear your story, so just listen. Rule number one: If you don't have a job, find one. Rule number two: You do your share of chores in the shelter. Tomorrow, look at the bulletin board, find your name and chores for the week. It changes weekly. Here's a list of the rest of the rules: Break even one, *one time*, and you're out of here." She looked at Jenny for a long time.

"Too bad your face ain't fixed yet. With your figure, we could use you as a greeter with the Christmas bells. You do look kinda pitiful, and Lord knows we need the money. This time of year, people need out of that cold. I'll ask around about jobs for you, but I warn you, people are gonna be suspicious about those bandages and you being young, skinny and downright frail-looking.

"My name is Helen," she continued. "I work from nine in the morning until six o'clock. When I'm off, Lizzie is in charge. You're too late today for breakfast."

"I'm not hungry, just tired. I'll go to my room now," Jenny said weakly, leaning on the desk for support.

Helen started to walk away and turned around. "Your room is four doors down on the left."

"Thank you."

Jenny opened the door to a gray room, just slightly larger than a closet. The one window was barred, and the one cot sat flush against the wall. The bedside table was scratched and stained, with a phone book under one leg for balance. A chest with five drawers occupied the back wall, and a worn straight chair faced the doorway. She felt grateful that the small bathroom was private. *Some of my torture is over. Now I can make some plans.*

Turning off the light, she crawled on top of the unmade cot and collapsed. *I will not surrender. In the morning, I will summon hope again. Now, today has passed. My life begins again tomorrow.*

+++

"Are you deaf? Get up and get busy. What the hell kind of place you think this is?" The tall, thin Negro woman shook Jenny's shoulder.

Jenny woke abruptly and jumped out of bed, screaming and shaking.

The woman backed out of the room. "Lizzie, Lizzie, come here!" she screamed.

Another Negro woman about Jenny's age came running. "What's the matter, Mae?"

"This whore tried to kill me. What's wrong with her? You're not supposed to let those crazy, white whores in here. Look at her. She's already been in a damn fight."

Jenny sat on the cot, trying to stop shaking.

The younger woman walked over. "Hi, I'm Lizzie." She smiled and sat in the chair. "Helen's out sick today, but she told me about you. That's Mae. She is so full of herself. Go on Mae, get out of here. Your mouth probably scared her to death, either that or your boney ass."

"This is the only place for me to stay right now," Jenny said keeping her eyes straight ahead.

"Don't worry about Mae." Lizzie leaned over and touched Jenny's hand. "We start work at five-thirty every morning, seven days a week. This shelter is supported by the church, and if they ever find us lazing around, they'll close it down without a second thought. So, go eat, get a mop and pail and clean the dining room. I'll check on some kind of paying job for you."

Jenny stood, and the weakness took over her body. Wobbling into the bathroom, she could feel the bandages sliding off her face. She closed the door, turned around, and faced the shattered mirror image, again. Slowly she slid to the floor. This time, there was no medication to ease the anguish.

Voices shook her into action. People were talking and walking outside the door.

Leaning against the wall for support, she rose, held onto the bathroom sink and stared into the mirror. With shaking hands, she gently touched her face. *My eyes, nose, and mouth are okay. The rest of my face is a roadmap of disconnected lines, scar tissue, and discolored pink skin. I have lost myself.*

A lonely tear escaped. Jenny felt the salty sting on her face, and gently wiped it away. After neatly rebandaging her face, she opened the door. Everything was quiet. *I need to eat something and obey these damn rules,* she reminded herself as she walked down the hall.

The dining room had space for three tables without tablecloths, with four chairs at each table. Gray walls held faded religious pictures. The area appeared empty, and the light bulb dangling from a cord showed her only a plate of doughnuts, a coffee pot, a jar of milk, paper cups and napkins on the table. Everything was quiet. She gently exhaled. *Everyone had gone to work, or to find work.*

"Hey."

Jenny stiffened, and her leg muscles tightened, her body poised to run.

"I said, Hey. Are you deaf as well as a mummy?" It came from a dark corner.

She froze, heart racing, fear in every inch of her body.

"What?" she stuttered, a little louder than she intended.

"Oh," the voice in the corner said. "Sorry, I thought you saw me."

"No, it's kind of dark away from the light in here."

"Well, come over and sit. I won't bite, and I hate sitting by myself."

Jenny placed a doughnut on a napkin and poured a cup of coffee, then approached the table, where she saw a white man, about forty years old, wearing a brown tweed suit. His dark brown hat had a wide brim and a wide band with a tiny feather, pulled low over his brow. He looked like a movie star.

She stared at him. He smiled and pushed out an empty chair with his foot.

Maybe he is a church deacon. Sliding into the chair, trying not to tremble, she smiled. *I really need to stay here, for now, at least. I have to make him like me.*

"Hi. My name is Sam, friends call me Sammy. That is, my lucky friends… What's your name?"

She cleared her throat. "I came in yesterday."

"You far away from home, or lost?"

She hesitated only for a moment. "Oh, no, well, yes, I mean, I was traveling with my boyfriend and we had a car accident. We got separated," she explained. "And we were taken to different hospitals. My name is Jenny."

"Where were you traveling from and where were you headed?"

The lies flowed easily. "We came from Arkansas and we were going to New York City. Maybe get married, after we found jobs."

"What kind of work did you plan to do in New York City?"

"He is very good with cars."

"Do you know where he is now?"

"No. But… we were starting to get on each other's nerves."

"Well, you need to make money to stay here, Jenny, and you can't stay here forever."

Was he really a church deacon? He asked a lot of questions. She was about to ask what he was doing here, when someone said her name loudly.

"Jenny Stone!" Lizzie approached the doorway, wringing her hands.

"What the hell do you think this is, a social club? Sam, this girl and I need to discuss her present living conditions, before you start in on your song and dance."

"Hey, watch your mouth, Lizzie. I give you a lot of slack, on account of your blind eye, but don't you go and get uppity with me."

He rose and laughed. "Good day, Lizzie. Good day Jenny Stone. I'll see you soon."

+++

"When can you take those rags off your face?" Lizzie barked, still pacing. "They're disgusting. Is there *really* something wrong with your face or are you just trying to hide from somebody?" Jenny jumped when Lizzie almost knocked a chair over.

"My face—no, nothing's wrong, but my wounds haven't healed yet, and it feels better with the bandages on."

"Okay, sister," Lizzie said, sitting down with Jenny and attempting a smile. She looked over her shoulder, made the sign of the cross, pressed a palm to her heart and exhaled. "I got a little work for you until your face is better. You go down to the Grape Tree office building, on the corner, at Twenty-Third and Central, at eight o'clock tomorrow night. You'll clean, sweep, mop and empty every trash can on the fourth floor. Check the bathroom for paper towels, toilet paper and soap. And don't forget, clean all four bathrooms."

Lizzie stood and motioned for Jenny to follow. She reached behind the desk. "Here's the key to the back door. It's marked with a janitor's sign. All the workers will be gone. They go home at five. Lock the door behind you. They don't want homeless people sleeping in the building. You'll work four hours each night. Your pay will be about five dollars a month. Any questions?" Lizzie asked in a calmer tone.

"No."

She wanted to know more about Sam, but decided to leave it alone for now.

Lizzie continued, "Mae cleans Monday and Friday. You clean Tuesday, Wednesday, and Thursday. They have a night watchman, named Harry. I've told him about your accident. I don't need his heart giving out at the sight of you with all that gauze on your face. Just do your job."

"Thank you, Lizzie." Jenny hoped she sounded grateful. "I'll do my best."

"You better, 'cause night jobs are all you gonna find with a face like yours.

"Well, I need to get back to work." Lizzie started to leave, then turned around. "By the way," her frown softened. "The Mission Thrift Store down the street has some clothes that might fit you. After you finish eating and do your chores, go down there and look around. Tell them I sent you."

Jenny cleaned the dining area and helped Lizzie with other chores.

"I'll go to the mission office for the forms for your work assignment," Lizzie announced. "You'll need the papers as proof to get your pay."

+++

Jenny finished the chores, put on her weathered black coat, which was tattered from daily wear, straightened the gauze mask on her face, and walked out of the gray mission shelter.

The icy wind penetrated her skin through her frayed coat. Never forgetting the rules of survival (*do, say, go, when, and where you are told*), she carefully stepped along the narrow, weed-lined sidewalk, and quickly walked three blocks. With only two blocks left to walk to the mission store, Jenny collided with a stone wall of a man.

"I'm sorry," she said through chattering teeth, and rushed to pull the black hood lower over her face.

"Oh, na," responded a deep thunderous voice.

She clenched her fists in her pockets and peeked out. She saw a big smile, black shirt with a white collar, and flaming red hair. She had stumbled into a priest.

"It's my fault, you see, lassie, I never be keeping my mind and body going in the same direction. Well, now. My name is Father

McPherson and goodness, my child, you look as if you've been in an accident."

"Yes, some time ago."

"Oh, my," said the priest. "We may see each other again. Now I better get moving. They'll be needing my services at the orphanage. We have a lot of the wee ones, especially lads." He tipped his hat and hurried down the street.

Jenny choked back tears. She called to the priest, "Please stop. Wait, please." Her words blew into the wind. He turned the corner and disappeared out of sight without hearing her plea.

"Orphanage, orphanage," her lips repeated. "What if Jet is in an orphanage? What if something happened to Ruth?" It was all too much for her. She burst into tears. Out of breath, leaning against a cold building, she forced her thoughts to the present. She had to survive *right now*. Nothing else was important.

With one hand, she touched the stinging ridges of exposed skin on her sensitive face. It made her feel nauseated. She stumbled the final two blocks to the mission store and pushed open the heavy door.

Then the warmth of the store, the countertop loaded with candy jars, and the short slim woman smiling behind the counter welcomed her. Jenny walked forward feeling lonely but hopeful.

The lady looked around the register. "What can I do for you?"

Her voice was soft and non—threatening. Taking a deep breath, Jenny answered, "Lizzie at the mission shelter told me to look for clothes here."

The lady waved her hand for Jenny to come forward.

"That's quite a large bandage," the lady commented, her kind words requiring no answer.

"You're tiny," the lady went on. "Some nice things came yesterday from a well—to-do family in Eastview. They have a girl about your size. Find something pretty. The boxes and racks of clothing are in back. If you need me, I'm Anna. What's your name, my dear?"

"Jenny Stone." She walked down the nearest aisle. *No more questions, please.*

Anna called to Jenny, "Try and find gloves; it's nasty outside without gloves. Take your time; today's my paperwork day."

Jenny blurted out, "I don't have any money now. I start work tomorrow."

Anna looked up. "Oh, honey, I should have told you. Today is discount shopping. You pay after your first paycheck for items today at discount prices."

Jenny looked through racks of clothes, boxes of shoes, and piles of sweaters, and began to relax. She was enjoying the little excursion. Her constant fright began to fade.

Two hours later, hungry and exhausted, with her shopping cart full, she approached the counter.

Anna removed her spectacles and placed the clothes on the counter. Jenny helped match the outfits as they folded the clothes.

"It looks great, the way you've matched the different pieces. Jenny, you have a knack for style. My goodness, child, if we had more in our budget, I'd ask them to bring you on. People need to look at whole *outfits*, instead of just mismatched odds and ends."

With all the clothes neatly folded, Anna placed them in a large bag.

"This will be too heavy for you," she warned Jenny.

"No, I can manage." She took the bag, gave Anna a hug and left, wearing her new gloves. She felt renewed by the clean, pretty clothes.

The sun cast shadows off the tall buildings. *Today's been a busy day. I hope Lizzie is off duty when I get back. This took longer than I thought. I'm still weak, and I missed supper.*

There were no streetlamps, but as darkness fell, the lights in some of the apartment buildings shone onto the sidewalk.

Three blocks from the shelter, she began to feel an overwhelming sense of being watched. *Don't look back. Don't feel afraid.* She pulled her shadow coat hood lower over her cold face.

Her legs ached and her stomach churned. She tightened her arms around the treasured bag of clothes and quickened her pace, hearing footsteps not far behind her. Trying not to panic, she thought of Father McPherson or someone else, hurrying home from work. *That's all it is. I'm sure of it.*

With two blocks to go, she turned the corner, and even with the cold wind, she distinctly heard footsteps.

Jenny's mind raced. The hell with bravery. She increased her steps to a slow trot, but the footsteps gained on her. Terrified, freezing, hands numb under the gloves, she let go of the bag, shaking uncontrollably. If those goons got their hands on her again… She stumbled forward, begging, "Please, let me die this time."

"Hey, hey, wait," yelled a male voice. "Jenny Stone, *wait,* stop."

Jenny slumped against the building, trying to clear her thoughts. *I know that voice.* She looked down the street.

Sam was putting the dropped clothes in the bag. He approached Jenny. "Why the hell are you running? You're not the only damn person allowed on this street!"

Breathless, fists clenched, Jenny shouted at Sam, "I don't know my way around here!" Anger and fear showed through her tear-filled eyes.

Sam saw the tears but said nothing and finished filling the bag. "I don't think they're damaged. I'll carry the bag. If you don't show up with these damn clothes, Helen will put a death wish on my head."

They walked in silence. Jenny hated Sam's presence beside her. He'd stolen her few precious moments of happiness and freedom.

Sam talked on as they walked. "How in the hell did you carry this? Thank God, you're not my problem."

They arrived at the steps of the mission. Sam gave Jenny the bag and tipped his hat, then walked away, head lowered, a fearless man.

"Oh." Helen stood staring; head held high, demanding attention. "You *did* come back. Lizzie mentioned you were going to get clothes. Did you tell Anna you're staying at the shelter?"

Jenny relaxed a little, rubbing her hands together to reduce the cold. "Yes, and the clothes are free until I get a paycheck."

Helen walked inside the hall toward the office, turned around and looked at Jenny. "Go put your clothes away, 'cause I got some talking and you got some listening to do. Hurry up; you already missed supper."

Jenny dropped the bag on the floor and dragged it to her room. She was dog-tired to the bone and fearful about leaving the shelter. Where would she go?

She rushed back to the lobby. Helen looked up and motioned her to the office. "I have good news and bad news." She noticed Jenny looking at the empty chair next to her. "Sit down." Jenny sat, relieved to be off her feet. "The good news is, you have a better-paying job offer. The bad news, well, in your case, it still could be good news, considering your face. The job is at night, in the Davis Library Archives. The resource director called. The job requires someone with a little education. You sound educated and you wrote on your job application that you attended school. Now, the question is, did you lie? I mean, can you read book titles and follow directions?"

"Yes, Helen, I can. Oh, a job with better pay!" She jumped up from the chair without realizing it and hugged herself.

"Hold on a minute," cautioned Helen. "Sit down and pay attention. I don't know much about the job except what the resource director said, so here goes. They're changing how they group the different sections according to, well, Lord, I forgot the exact instructions. All the information is in here." She handed an envelope to Jenny and added, "I guess what's important is, how you look won't matter. You'll work from 10:00 pm to 6:00 am. Since you live and eat here, for now, use some of the money for personal care stuff. Your wages will be about ten dollars a month. The Queen of Angels Catholic Church is next door to the library

This better work. Mae doesn't like you, told me that you gave her the creeps and you would be in her way with the cleaning job."

After those brief comments, Jenny took the envelope and returned to her room, trying to process this roller—coaster day.

She slept for two hours. Then despite her weariness, she prepared for her shower. During her shopping spree, she'd found a black lace-net veil. It was far more appropriate for her damaged face. Resting on the toilet, with great effort, she removed the bandages, subdued a flash of nausea at the sight, and put the veil on. She secured it with a black headband and elastic strap.

Immediately, she looked much more presentable.

If the truth will kill me, I will choose to lie. From this day forward, I will have a serious skin condition. No one need ever know what happened.

Survival was important to Jenny, and now, security was essential.

+++

Helen and Lizzie had been maids for the church. When the mission shelter opened, they cleaned and asked to take on more duties. Until Jenny arrived, the women coming and leaving were Negroes, beaten prostitutes, homeless and hopeless.

After a confrontation with Helen, Mae left one night and never returned. Helen and Lizzie decided they needed help. Women were living from shelter to shelter. Since Prohibition, the government decided to tax beer and wine. Many underground clubs existed, created by gangsters. A lot of women depended on those clubs for work.

Women had won the right to vote in 1920, but this meant little to a shelter resident. The Great Depression left many waiting in line at soup kitchens, mostly men without jobs. The women were ignored. They received the leftovers, if any remained.

Helen met with the church priest to discuss Jenny's situation. They decided to allow Jenny to stay and assist, under Helen's supervision.

"Jenny, you're becoming a mission pro," Lizzie joked. Two years ago, Jenny had entered the mission shelter. Immediately with her first pay, she put herself on a tight budget, buying Lifebuoy soap (seventeen cents for three bars), Pepsodent toothpaste (twenty-seven cents per tube), Octagon laundry soap (twenty-two cents per package) and Noxzema cream (forty-nine cents) for the sensitive facial scars. This enabled her to save about half her paycheck each month. She did buy a little more clothing, volunteering for Anna, helped shave down the cost. *I will move forward and find Jet,* she dreamed in her spare time. *I probably have enough money now to rent an apartment, maybe not enough for food and clothes from the store. But I feel safe here, for now.* She had no dreams beyond those thoughts.

Jenny prepared the orientation sessions for all new drop-ins before she went to her library job. She felt peaceful going to Mass on Sunday. All the women wore something on their heads, mostly veils. She experienced gentle touching feelings of long-ago memories. *This is my kind of place, a lovely place.*

Father McPherson noticed the young veiled woman several times at Mass. At each service, she sat alone, head lowered. She never received communion. When anyone attempted to start a conversation, she would leave by the nearest exit.

+++

One Sunday, a few weeks later, Jenny watched numbly, her face expressionless behind the veil. She waited patiently, rehearsed her words carefully. As the priest approached, Jenny remained in his path. She offered a trembling handshake.

I will risk this for my son. I will ask for a miracle. It's been too much time without answers.

"I need, I mean, a friend of mine," Jenny chose her words carefully, "wants to know if one of the boys in the orphanage is named Jet?"

"Well, hello. It's kind of you to ask, my dear." His Irish brogue was as thick as the first time they'd spoken. "Maybe a little more information? A description of the lad would be helpful."

"Black hair, beautiful blue eyes, almost eight years old and so much energy," Jenny responded in a tight, high-pitched voice. *God, please make this happen,* she prayed. *I don't want to live without Jet.* She fell silent.

The Irish priest placed a hand on her shoulder. "We have no such lad at the orphanage, but I will be alert for this boy. How would I get in touch with your friend?"

Jenny folded her hands as if praying. With a falsely confident smile, she requested the priest report any information to her. "The mother will probably leave the mission soon. I promised I'd keep in touch with her." She spoke slowly, exuding calm and focus.

With a quick wave, thinking worst-case scenarios, she smoothed her veil, wanting to be somewhere else. *But for better or worse, I feel kindness in his voice.*

+++

Sam visited the shelter every two weeks for the stress-free conversation. He began to want to learn what was on Jenny's mind. He enjoyed her laughter at his silly jokes. It gave him temporary respite from a life of shameful secrets.

After several visits, Sam realized that Jenny believed he was one of the deacons of the shelter and quickly set her straight. Otherwise, he told her little about himself, and she told him nothing about herself. 'No personal sharing' became their unspoken rule.

The relationship was unusual, but non-threatening. Sam knew Jenny never considered him anything other than a male acquaintance, someone to talk about day-to-day events. He didn't delude himself that she would confide in him.

When she was unaware, he looked closely at her veiled face and knew she was extremely disfigured. *God, she must have been beautiful, a perfect body, slim, with curves in just the right places. If her face had matched her body...* He quickly put the thought out of his mind.

He knew a lot of women, for all the wrong reasons. He had no desire for a long-term relationship. His dangerous world could cause trouble for any woman.

Sam asked Jenny to attend a masquerade party at the Blue Moon Club. "You can wear the veil," he said, "and meet some friends of mine. It will do you good to go out. Think about it. You could wear your veil and not be self-conscious about your appearance. Everyone will be wearing a mask of sorts."

+++

After analyzing the pros and cons, Jenny made up her mind to go to the party. She *did* want to get out and have fun. It had been way too long. *Maybe this will be my chance. At least, I won't be alone.*

In a state just approaching bliss, she set off to the mission store for a possible costume. She found Anna in the back trying to lift some heavy boxes.

"Wait, Anna! Let me help. You shouldn't be doing that."

"Oh!" replied Anna, "And I suppose all your 100 pounds is gonna do it?"

"Yes. Give them to me one at a time," Jenny snapped. She climbed the ladder. Anna handed the boxes to her. "I'm going to a masquerade party with Sam. What should I go as?"

"Well now, let me think. I saw some bright, odd clothes with tiny sequin patterns on them. I think you'd make a beautiful Egyptian dancing girl. Get down off that ladder, and let's shop."

+++

Sam arrived at the shelter the following Saturday wearing a Yankee baseball uniform with his favorite player, Babe Ruth's, number—three--displayed on the back of the jersey. Lizzie was working a double shift at the desk. She looked up and frowned.

"Hi, Lizzie," Sam said. Lizzie looked at Sam a long time, slowly and carefully choosing her words.

"Sam, you know I'm afraid of you and what I think you do. I haven't said a word to Jenny. That child has been hurt enough. Can't you just leave her be?"

"Lizzie, I'm her friend," Sam said. "If she wants to go out and have fun, what damn business is it of yours?"

Lizzie opened her mouth to speak. Then she put both hands on her face in disbelief.

Jenny walked toward them. They watched in amazement.

"I've died and gone to heaven," Sam exclaimed. "You are a vision, Jenny Stone, a beautiful dream."

Jenny had secured the veil over her face with a jeweled head band around her forehead. She wore white silk pants and a matching top with red sequins sewn on the shoulders.

"I'm an Egyptian dancer," she announced, immensely pleased, displaying her ballet slippers while twirling around to show off the costume. "I found all of this at the store with Anna. She altered them to fit me."

"You look like a movie star," Lizzie said.

"Sam, are you sure it looks okay for tonight?" Jenny asked.

"Okay? Honey, it's more than okay. It's perfect! *You're* perfect! Let's get out of here." He grabbed Jenny's hand, turned and winked at Lizzie.

"Jenny," Lizzie cautioned, "no alcohol. You can't come in here if you've been drinking."

"Tell Lizzie bye, Jenny," Sam said. He hurried her toward the car. They laughed and drove away.

+++

The Blue Moon nightclub jammed over 150 patrons in the downtown club for special events. Cars parked bumper to bumper on both sides of Patton Street.

"Oh, Sam, I don't think I can do this."

"Yes, you can," Sam said. "You're with me, and nobody will bother you."

Sam parked the car, and together, they entered the private, members-only club. The party was going full blast.

In the ballroom, all heads turned toward Jenny and Sam. She grasped Sam's arm and steadied herself.

"Didn't I tell you not to worry?" Sam patted Jenny's hand and guided her through the crowd to a table at the back of the room.

The club entertained a paradise atmosphere. The guests entered into an exquisite wrap-around balcony, decorated in multi-colored flowers, twin staircases that flowed down each side, and chandeliers that lit the room with fairy-tale lighting.

Several of Sam's friends, male and female, stopped by their table, all wearing costumes and masks. Jenny became less anxious. A round of drinks arrived and after some teasing, playful remarks, Jenny enjoyed a mixed drink, which someone called it a Blue Moon special.

"It tastes like bubblegum," Jenny said. She noticed Sam was served orange juice.

The music started; Jenny relaxed. Sam gently pulled her onto the beautiful marble dance floor. She loved the swing dance.

Then, the music slowed, and they waltzed to *"Seems Like Old Times"* by the Royal Canadians. She looked around at the floor and ceiling mirrors, closed her eyes in bliss, *I look beautiful.*

She leaned into Sam's frame and placed her head softly on his shoulder. *Sometimes in life, we just need to be held, to make you feel you matter.*

Before midnight, Sam cautioned Jenny it was time to leave; everyone would remove their masks at twelve. She nodded and they negotiated the crowd toward the door. Several men jokingly attempted to stop them, but no one persisted; no one made Sam do anything Sam did not want to do.

He turned at the door and said, "Good night, ladies and gentlemen, for now. I am responsible for this young lady, and I'll be as good as my word." He tipped his hat.

As they crossed the street, a police car sped toward them.

"Stop right there," said a cop, looking out the car window. "I believe we have a nice back seat for the lady and a back alley for the cockroach," he laughed. Sam walked over, leaned down to the window and said something.

The cop sputtered, "Sam, I didn't know it was you. Sam, you gotta believe me. Come on Sam, give me a break."

Sam straightened up and walked back to where Jenny stood.

"Come on," he said. He drove Jenny quickly to the shelter, said good night, and drove off.

Jenny stepped softly to her room. She noticed Lizzie's light and tiptoed past, just as Lizzie opened the door.

"You get in that room and get some sleep, Jenny." Without another word, Lizzie stepped back inside and closed the door. Jenny heard Lizzie say, "Thank you, Lord."

+++

Days came and went. Sam did not return to the shelter. Jenny waited for him, increasingly concerned. *Had her friend disappeared, and chosen not to tell her why? Was she only someone he had to pity?*

She questioned Lizzie and Helen, but they shook their heads and told her to mind her own business.

She missed their conversations. He respected her feelings and never asked about her past.

+++

Jenny took short walks in the neighborhood. When it was her turn to cook, she enjoyed going to the little fish market, and stopping by the park that wasn't far from the shelter.

Today was mild for mid-December. To pass the time, she decided to walk to the park. It was only three o'clock, plenty of time before she would go to her night job.

Finding her favorite bench empty, she sat and watched the children swing and play on the slides.

Then a loud squeal jolted her out of her thoughts. A little boy, about eight years old, raced in front of her, tripped and fell. Jenny got up and hurried over to him.

Bending down, she asked, "Are you all right? Let me help you up."

The little boy screamed, "Mommy, Mommy, help me, help me!" A woman ran over, followed by several other people. Jenny moved back as the woman pushed past her.

"Darling, it's all right. Mommy is here." She looked at Jenny and started shouting. "Get away from my son! Get away from him."

Jenny felt her face. Her veil had fallen off when she ran to help the boy. With the woman screaming, Jenny snatched up the veil and left the park running, hiding her face, feeling her heart would break.

+++

Christmas came and went. Jenny was depressed and miserable. She had the flu twice, and barely spoke to anyone. She hadn't realized when Sam said good-bye after the party, he wasn't coming back.

Three months later, as the first blooms of spring colored the landscape, Sam returned.

Jenny came out of her room and heard Lizzie and Sam talking.

"Oh, Sam, Sam!" Jenny ran down the hall and threw her arms around his neck. "Sam, you came back!"

Silently, she prayed, *please stay*. As usual, Jenny didn't question him about his whereabouts.

"Well," Sam exclaimed, "I'll go away more often, if this is my homecoming. Even Lizzie said hello to me!"

"Well," Lizzie smiled, "you sure do make Jenny happy. She's been like a little sad puppy around here, not eating, wasting away to skin and bone. If you can change that, then I guess I can say hello."

Jenny and Sam fell into a comfortable routine, now that he was back. They enjoyed talking, going to the Blue Moon, having a few drinks and dancing. She always wore her veil, creating suspicion, though no one dared to comment.

On one relaxing night after the club closed, Jenny sang a short song for Sam and his friends. *There is so much that I want to share with Sam. Maybe one day…*

Her veil became part of her style. No one questioned it. Everyone had something to hide, anyway.

"I'll call this place the Peek-A-Boo Club," she whispered to Sam. Everyone seemed to peek out from under a hat, a veil, or a pair of sunglasses. They all kept their heads down, but not Sam. He was handsome and confident, always smiling, holding his head high. He bought everyone a round of drinks or paid a taxi to take someone home who was too drunk to drive. Yes, Sam had many friends at the club.

Sometimes, a guy named Charlie drove the car. They went from club to club, meeting friends and dancing. Other times, Sam sent Charlie into a club with a message, and they stayed in the car.

On two nights, Jenny missed work, complaining of nausea all day. She and Sam had gone out on each Friday and Saturday night. During these special nights, she breathed deeply, and squeezed her eyes at her small steps of joy to push back her fright of violence.

She had such a great time, but then, three weeks passed with no word from Sam. *How can he keep hurting me, or does he even care?*

+++

Jenny went to the library each night. She enjoyed her job and knew everything about the library. While she worked, she removed her veil and felt free as a bird. Often, she hurried through her chores and spent time reading.

Tonight, she had an idea to check out a book, maybe about New Jersey, not stop until she had read something about every state in the USA.

I'll fill out a library card just like everyone and then I'll check out my book.

She found the index card file, completed a library card and started to place the card in the box. Let's see, Stallman, Stevenson, Stillman...

Jenny froze, holding in a scream.

Stillman, Ruth.

"Oh God," she said. She removed the card and read, "Stillman, Ruth, 106 Maple Avenue, telephone 212-6789".

Jenny's heart raced, and she pressed the card to her chest. *Ruth?*

After a few minutes, she took a piece of paper and wrote down the information about Ruth Stillman. While she copied the information, Jenny noticed the title of the book Ruth Stillman had checked out, "*BECOMING A BOY SCOUT*".

There could be no doubt. This was her friend. *Please God, let the boy be my son.*

She trembled and placed her new library card, Stone, Jenny, behind Stillman, Ruth.

For days, Jenny was beside herself, pacing in her room, walking with no idea where she was going. So many thoughts raced through her mind.

Ruth had a son? He must *be Jet. What had happened to Jet? What to do with the information she'd discovered? No one besides Ruth must know the secret that would keep her son alive.*

Finally, hoping and praying, she opened the index file box, just to make sure it wasn't a dream or her imagination. *Let me just find her street.* Jenny knew where to find the information in the library's city map section and immediately found Maple Street, the 100 block, two blocks from North Central Hospital. Yes, this Ruth Stillman was her friend.

Jenny always stayed in her neighborhood during the day. She was comfortable and safe on her streets. Today, she decided to take a taxi just to see Maple Street.

"Where to?" said the cab driver.

"106 Maple Street."

She looked out the window as they traveled into the older neighborhoods, where well-kept sidewalks enclosed houses, not apartments, and beautiful oak trees looked over green grassy lawns with white picket fences. The sun was setting, and every house had a light on. Lace curtains dressed the dining room windows. At one house, several people sat at the table, laughing and eating.

"Lady, this is 106 Maple Street."

She handed money to the driver and stepped out. He drove off.

Jenny stood mesmerized. *As long as I stand here, I have a past. I was loved. Being this close to the two of you answers so many of my questions. I'll pretend that I'm sitting at that table, listening to you. "Pass the biscuits, please, Momma."*

That same love will keep me away from you. I will protect you at any cost.

A nicely-dressed man and woman approached her.

"Are you lost?" the man asked, rather abruptly.

"No. No, I thought this was the right house, but I was mistaken," Jenny replied.

"You should keep on walking," he said sternly. The woman pulled on his arm, and they hastened away.

Jenny overheard the woman say, "When we get to the next corner, find a policeman. Did you look at her clothes? For two cents, I'd have snatched that veil off her face. That woman must clean or something for her. We've had two break-ins this month on this block. We must do something about this. You find a policeman now, Frank."

"Okay," Frank said, and they rushed up the street, looking back several times.

Jenny shook her fists in the air and walked quickly in the opposite direction, remembering the hospital was two blocks away. If a policeman came by, a woman wearing a veil would be easily identified. She dashed into the main entrance of the hospital and went immediately to the women's bathroom, where she stayed for over an hour. *I do not have the strength to walk to the shelter and damn it all, I am not riding with another smart-ass taxi driver.* She found a phone booth outside and without a second thought, called Sam. *Thank God, he was home.*

Sam drove to the hospital's main entrance. Twenty minutes later, he opened the car door for Jenny. She had been crying.

"Jenny, what happened? Are you hurt? In trouble? What are you doing here? Please, let me help."

"It's none of your goddamn business, Sam. Just take me to the Blue Moon... You got a cigarette?"

"Since when do you smoke?"

"Since right now."

Sam lit a cigarette and handed it to her. She inhaled. The tobacco burned deeply into her lungs. Following a bout of coughing, she took several deep breaths, and started to relax.

Sam drove to the club. Jenny demanded whiskey. Sam ordered orange juice. She drank quickly, letting the liquid flow throughout her shattered body.

Sam went to the bar and brought a full bottle back with him. "Hell, if it's that bad, you better drown it with this." He asked no questions; fearful of the answers.

After several hours of drinking, Jenny was drunk. It was one A.M., and the bar was closing. Sam could not take her to the shelter in that condition. He must decide.

"Jenny," Sam whispered. "Jenny, let's go." He drove to his apartment. Jenny ask no questions. The whiskey drowned her memories, and she was glad.

+++

Sam never entertained in his home. He had nice, private living arrangements, an expensive car, and tailor-made clothes. Being alone and careful kept him alive. Tonight, he had no choice.

Jenny sat on the edge of the bed. He removed her shoes. She fell on the bed. He pulled the covers over her and attempted to remove the veil. She put her hand over it and turned her face into the pillow.

"Well, Jenny Stone, it *must* be bad, if you can be blind drunk and *still* manage to hide your face. Good night, now." Turning out the light, Sam took a blanket and pillow to sleep on the couch.

Jenny woke at 6 a.m. Her eyes hurt. Her mouth tasted like cotton, and her head felt like a boulder. Nausea took over. She needed the bathroom.

She noticed light outside the door and managed to stand, sliding her hand against the wall to take a few steps. The light came from a bathroom down the hall.

She used the toilet and stood holding onto the sink. The cold water chilled her body, and a wave of nausea hit; the bathroom began to spin. She fainted, face forward onto the floor.

Sam woke to the noise. After a few minutes, he realized the events of the night. He jumped off the couch, raced to the bedroom and found the bed empty, then noticed the light in the hall bathroom. When he pushed against the door, it didn't budge.

"Jenny, Jenny, open the door." No answer.

Frightened, he forced the door open. Jenny lay almost in front of the door, face down, her veil nowhere in sight. He bent down and turned Jenny over.

The sight sent a shock through his body. Her face looked like a jigsaw puzzle. Sam was horrified. He couldn't stare at her and touch her at the same time.

"Shit," he muttered. She felt small in his arms as he carried her to the bed. Her veil lay on the pillow.

He placed it over her face, making sure the little elastic band was secured under her neck. Then, he drank three cups of the strongest coffee he could get down his throat without vomiting.

He had seen Jenny lift the veil slightly, while eating and drinking. She was careful with her secret. He hoped she wouldn't realize he'd found her unveiled.

He knew she had been in an awful accident. Sam was still shaking from the sight. She looked like a creature out of a freak show. After all his time with street whores, he knew what a deliberate mutilation looked like. This was the work of the devil himself, not accidental.

Why? And why had whoever did this let her *live*. Or did they? Had they tried to kill her? Did they know she was alive? Where did it happen? When? And what happened at North Central Hospital that had made her so angry?

He was thinking hard, while pacing the living room.

"Sam, Sam, Jenny called from the bedroom. "Sam, are you there?"

Sam slowly walked in. "Oh, Jenny, you're awake. I slept like a dead man. Why are you up so early?"

"Lizzie's going to kill me. I can't get out of this bed. Every time I try, the room starts spinning."

"I'll make coffee," said Sam, realizing thankfully that Jenny did not remember the bathroom incident. "Just stay where you are. I'm not in good shape, either."

He poured a cup of coffee, walked into Jenny's room and placed the cup on the table, forcing himself not to look at her.

"Oh, Sam," Jenny said, as he was going out the door. "Could I please have a cigarette?"

"Hooked already? Sure, there's a pack and a lighter in the drawer of the bedside table. Just use that ashtray. We don't want a fire here."

When Lizzie or Helen finds out, it'll be a mess. Sam wished this hadn't happened, but no way to go back now. He must take Jenny back to the shelter.

Sam brought in two cups of strong, black coffee, propped her up with pillows, and gave her a cup. Both noticed their hands were trembling.

"Jenny, drink the coffee. I'm going out for awhile. Don't leave, and don't answer the door."

"Don't worry, I'm going back to sleep." Jenny closed her eyes.

Sam went directly to the shelter, hoping Lizzie was on duty. He could frighten Lizzie into forgetting Jenny was missing.

Instead, Helen sat at the desk, completing paperwork. He didn't know Helen well, just enough not to try to push her around.

He walked over and said, "Hi, I'm Sam, a friend of Lizzie's and Jenny's."

Helen looked Sam in the eye. "If you're Jenny's friend, can you explain where she was last night? She didn't work, and she isn't here."

Sam wasn't prepared for this. He said nothing.

"So, do you know, Mr. Sam?" she snapped.

Sam knew better than to lie to this woman. "Well, Jenny got sick. That's the truth."

Helen walked out from behind the desk and stood looking at him.

"I swear," Sam said, and put his hand over his heart.

"No swearing, Mr. Sam. You'd either better leave or start talking sense," Helen said.

"All right. Jenny is sick. I picked her up at North Central Hospital last night. She was too tired to work, and my apartment was close by. I slept on the couch; Jenny wouldn't have it any other way."

Helen looked hard at him for a moment. "You may be talking the truth," she said finally. "But breaking the rules has consequences. We told her that right at the start.

You tell Jenny she has no job at the library now. She cannot come back to the shelter. Her things are in that box." She pointed to a corner. "Take them, and don't come back here. There's nothing we can do. You should have considered this before you let her stay at your place last night."

"Come on," pleaded Sam. "Give her a break! You know it's not easy for Jenny. She can't make it on her own."

Helen shook her head. "And why didn't Jenny at least call here this morning?"

"I told you, she's sick."

"I'm sorry," Helen said. "I really tried to help her. I hope you will, too."

Sam began moving toward the box in the corner. "Just remember, whatever happens, you didn't give her a second chance."

"Do I need to call the police?" Helen reached for the phone.

"I'm going. Thanks for nothing."

Sam left as Lizzie walked up.

"Helen, you fussing at somebody?" Lizzie asked. "I heard a man talking, but I heard you louder."

"Jenny has gone and moved in with Sam. Lord help her."

"Damn!" Lizzie said. "Oh! Sorry. That Sam is up to no good. Jenny is gonna regret the day she met him."

"Stop talking about it," Helen ordered.

Lizzie knew they would miss Jenny more than either would admit.

Chapter Nine

The Friend

Driving back to the apartment, his mind racing, Sam knew he needed a plan. *Any other woman, I would have screwed her, thrown her out, with no regrets. This time, I broke my rules.*

Jenny is not like other women. She's a friend, and I need a friend. Though I don't need the burden of this woman. I'll tell her to get out and get on with her life. Hell no, I couldn't do that to her. Even the thought *of her on the streets makes me sick.*

I'll wait till she's ready. When she's ready, Jenny will tell me her secret, and I'll help her.

He turned on the radio to ease his thoughts.

Okay, for a day or two, the couch is comfortable. Jenny's talking more freely. Yeah, I'll let her stay for two days. Then it's good-bye, Jenny, and good luck.

+++

Eight months later, Sam and Jenny were still together in his apartment. He travelled out of the country. She stayed home. More and more, she used vodka to get through the day.

He asked no questions; she gave no answers.

Sam was becoming a nervous wreck, smoking four to five packs of cigarettes daily. He hardly slept, and often left the apartment, abruptly, without a word. She no longer prepared meals. Sam didn't eat, anyway; he claimed he wasn't hungry. Several times when he came home, Jenny was too drunk to notice him. She knew he wanted to escape the trap of his life with her.

Tonight, will be another evening from hell. She took another drink to escape her sadness.

Sam finished dressing to go out. He no longer asked her to go with him.

"Sam," Jenny slurred his name, as he walked out of the bathroom. "Wait for me." She stumbled across the bedroom. "I'm going to the club."

Sam reached for his tie. Jenny was still in her slip, a glass of vodka in her hand.

"The hell you are. Look at you. You're a hopeless drunk. People don't like being around a drunk freak."

"Damn you, Sam!" she screamed.

"They're your words. I'm just agreeing with you. There's nothing left of the old Jenny." Sam tied his tie and used his handkerchief to wipe down his sweating brow.

"Then I want to die, Sam," she said, putting her arms around him. She hid her face in his shoulder, and he held her in his arms.

"I know baby," he said softly. "You got a bum rap, but living with me is not working. We're dying a slow death. You have to face the real world, honey, and take what you can from it."

"Please Sam, just tonight. Let me go out with you. I can't stay alone. I won't get in your way. Please, or I'm going to lose my mind."

Sam let go of Jenny. *God, if she only knew what Tony and I do. Maybe, if I tell her, she'd hate me and run like hell. Save herself. Of course, if I did tell her, Tony would kill us both.* Sam lit a cigarette and inhaled deeply.

"Jenny, come over here." He gave her the cigarette. She stood before him, waiting, hopeful. After a moment, he went into the bedroom and returned with her veil. "Here, put this on." He took her glass and cigarette.

As always, she did what he told her to do. Jenny knew that Sam cared for her. She believed he'd never hurt her. *I am safe here.*

"Now, take your clothes off," Sam said. Jenny did not respond. "Here, drink this." He gave her the glass.

She drank it and laughed. "You're joking, right?"

"No, I've known you for a long time, and I want to see the rest of the package."

"No. Sam, it's not just my face they butchered, it was all of me." The sadness brought tears.

He held her, with as much understanding and compassion as he could convey. "Well then," he said, "*I'll* take *my* clothes off."

She looked at him through her veil. *There are times when I believe in a future. I even choose to believe in the present, this moment.*

"Then let me help you, Sam." Slowly, Jenny unbuttoned his shirt, unfastened his belt.

"Now, Sam do not move." She knew Sam would not want her to stop.

Excitement led to abandonment. She unzipped his pants and ran her hands from his nipples across his chest, down his sides and back to the hair on his groin. He lifted himself and she slid his clothing down, kissing his nipples through her veil.

She reached up and closed his eyes, gently and kissed each eyelid.

Then the soft whisper. "Don't you do anything. I will take care of you, always." She slid one hand around his arousal, then her other hand found his mouth and her two fingers slowly entered. At the same time, she slowly used her tongue to wet his maleness. When Sam tried to touch her body, she stiffened and moaned. Gently, her fingers left his mouth, as she surrounded his erection and took him, using her hands tenderly to push him into her mouth.

His entire body convulsed. She released his engorged organ, and it emptied into her with a series of spasms. She brushed his limp member with feather kisses. Reaching up, she took Sam's hands and felt tremors of desire enter her body. She squeezed, moaned, forgetting the world outside. *I am still alive. I'm a woman.* A feeling of pure joy filled her body.

Jenny stood, kissed Sam on the forehead and poured herself another vodka. She felt desire and strength and hope for the future.

+++

Sam was breathless, sweat dripped from his body. He adjusted his clothing, feeling dizzy.

"Unbelievable." He put his head in his hands, almost sobbing. *What in hell just happened?*

Jenny sat quietly. *This time, I made my own rules. This time, it was magic, the way lovemaking should be.* She was frightened and terribly excited.

"I'm going out." He grabbed his coat without looking at her and practically ran out of the building to his car. *She is my friend and my lover.* Joy and desire flooded his body.

Jenny watched as Sam drove away.

She'd felt something long forgotten and fell asleep thinking of what she'd done and how wonderful she felt, doing it again, at long last.

PART
TWO

CHAPTER TEN

The Family

After Jenny's first lovemaking with Sam, they avoided each other except for a few passing words. Sam ached for Jenny to touch him, but he didn't know if she regretted what they'd done.

Several weeks later, she responded to his hug and kiss on the cheek. This led, inevitably, to a new and destructive habit.

With Jenny intoxicated and Sam now drinking, they began fantasy sexual rituals, where Sam was a lost stranger and Jenny the beautiful Egyptian princess who came to rescue him.

He brought her new costumes. She dressed up and pretended for him. Without saying it in words, they knew this dream world removed barriers for both of them. Sam began to spend more and more time with Jenny at the apartment. They drove into the country for picnics. The following week, he surprised her with a movie date.

+++

When Sam was in town, he reported to Anthony Salvadore weekly. His life depended upon promptness where Anthony Salvadore was concerned.

Today, Sam drove to the huge mansion for a 'family meeting', where the butler opened the door.

Sam went to the billiard room, as usual. Six guys were already there. They greeted each other as friends, smoked cigars, and ate from the platters of food on the bar.

An hour later, Anthony Salvadore entered the room, followed by his two gorilla bodyguards. He walked deliberately around the room, shook hands and patted shoulders.

Leaning close to Sam's ear, he whispered, "Gotta talk to you later, Sammy." he gave Sam a tight squeeze and gently touched Sam's face with his fist.

"Sit, sit everybody! Family don't stand around. Everybody here?" Mr. Salvadore laughed, and with a look, silently ordered everyone to laugh. They did.

"Let's get down to business. Marty's trying to move in on the East Side. He's bought the Cuban gang. They're popping anyone who nods the wrong way.

I been doing a lotta thinking about how hard I been working all my life, how I got where I am. I never let any moron take what belonged to me. Now, first, I need to know, are you going to let some Cuban assholes take that from us?"

"No, no way, they have to go through hell first." Everyone nodded and shouted obedience and loyalty.

"Now, listen," Anthony Salvadore said, looking straight at Sam. Sam started to speak, just as Anthony Salvadore picked up a bottle of gin and threw it at him. He ducked; the bottle crashed against the wall. Tony looked hard at Sam.

"Shut up and listen, Sam. That last load of whores from China, they're sick. All they been good for since they got here is to cost me money. What in hell did you give them on the way over?" He stood up. "Let me tell all of you something. There is trouble in this family, and *I'm going to fix it.*" He started pointing at the men, and each man in turn reported on his territory: Gambling, entertainment, prostitution, alcohol, illegal trade, drugs, all connected to millions of dollars funneled to Anthony Salvadore. Cops bribed, storekeepers beaten, murders, all nice and legal, no one cared.

"Now," Tony continued, "I need all business on the East Side reporting to me. Speedy," he said to a tall man wearing glasses. "I need the books Marty keeps in the Portland warehouse. Can you do that?"

"Yes, boss. I'll talk to Charlie."

"And Speedy," Mr. Salvadore added, "leave everyone speechless, okay?" All the men laughed, even Sam. The meeting continued for over four hours. Finally, everyone else left.

Sam remained sitting at the far end of the room. He lit a cigarette. Anthony Salvadore walked over and sat in a huge black chair across from Sam.

"Well, Sam, who is she? Where is she? And what the fuck is going on?"

Sam looked at his friend and boss for a moment.

Sam began, "You're like my older brother. We operate the biggest and toughest crime mob in the State of New York. Nothing will come between us. We cover each other's back and owe our lives to each other.

Tony, there's a girl, it's not what you think, she really is just a friend. She's living with me until she can find work. She got tossed out of a women's shelter, and it was my fault. She's a classy girl and believe me, she has a past she doesn't talk about and the cops are not friends of hers."

"Well Sammy, bring her around, let me meet this 'classy girl'." Sam knew this was not the time to say no to Tony, especially after he'd loused up that last load of workers.

"Sure, Tony."

"Now Sammy, talk to me about the Chinese whores. I got a company in need of about twenty in two weeks. Get them fixed. Are you introducing them to the best life can offer?" Sam knew a lot about drugs, and he knew enough never to use himself. On the other hand, he sure knew how to make anyone else fall in love with the stuff.

"They'll be ready. Listen, Tony, about Jenny. I want you to take it easy on her. She's lived a hard life, and it shows."

"What the hell are you talking about, Sammy? The fellows told me she was a knockout. You hiding something from me?"

"Well, as a matter of fact, Jenny *is* hiding something. From everybody but me," said Sam.

"You gonna tell me or do I have to find out for myself?" Tony persisted. Sam described Jenny's mutilated face and body to him.

When Sam finished talking, Tony was quiet. Violence was a huge part of his life, but to disfigure a woman's body for pleasure was both sick and disturbing.

Tony stood up. "Good God, why didn't they just kill her?"

"She doesn't know," Sam answered. "In fact, as far as they know, she *is* dead. And she likes it that way."

The two men sat in silence for awhile. They'd grown up together, poor, with cruel fathers and abused mothers. They put little time or effort into school; they were street smart. Every day, your life was in your hands.

+++

During the next three months, Sam went to China often, for weeks at a time. He needed the time to mask the revenge taken on Jenny's tormentors.

He used mob connections to locate the two evil brutes who had beaten her, and made sure he had the revenge he wanted, confirmed by a newspaper clipping mailed to him afterward, that described a mob rival execution.

A homeless man found two unidentified men near a warehouse. Toes, fingers and teeth were missing. Their bodies were slashed repeatedly, with barely any flesh left on their bones.

They couldn't hurt Jenny anymore, and he would never have to worry about it again.

+++

After several interruptions in the overseas business, Sam left for China and remained for four months. Jenny decided to drain the last drop of joy from whatever time she had left. Sober, she dressed in a yellow suit with a pale-yellow veil; she thought it gave her a Cinderella look.

She brushed her hair, flipped it back. She found a wide plastic belt that accented her thin figure. *When Sam returns, if he* ever *returns, I may have faded out of his life. So tonight, I'll celebrate our freedom. Now, Sam, you can* have your life back.

She walked into the club with her head held high and put a little swivel in her steps as she made her way to the back table.

A few men whistled. They were quickly hushed by their girlfriends. Jenny ordered her usual bottle and flirted with a bald, fat man, a first-time customer. They danced on the dimly-lit floor, and the rat was all over her.

+++

Speedy knew he had to avoid trouble. He approached the table. "Jenny, you about ready to go home? Sam expects you tonight."

"Not going home tonight, not ever going home. I don't have a home."

"Good," the bald man said. "Little girlie, you can go home with me."

"Now, that will be just fine," she said, emptying her glass.

Speedy reached over and took the bottle. "That's enough, Jenny, let's go."

"Just a damn minute, asshole. She's going with me, or are you deaf?" the bald guy blurted out.

Speedy turned his head to the right, and with one quick motion, two bouncers each took one of the fat man's arms. They left in a hurry, with the man's feet barely touching the floor.

"Jenny," Speedy whispered, "Mr. Salvadore is upstairs waiting for Sam. I think I better see you home…" Before he could finish the sentence, Jenny interrupted.

"Mr. Salvadore, Mr. Salvadore – I'm sick and tired of Mr. Salvadore. I don't even think there *is* a Mr. Salvadore." Jenny bolted from the room and stumbled up the stairs.

She ran down the hall and burst into a room marked OFFICE. A man about forty-five years old, tan, with graying hair, sat in a huge brown leather office chair.

"What the hell!" he said, jumping up. Jenny just stood there. Speedy ran up behind her.

"I'm sorry, Mr. Salvadore. This is Sam's girl. She's all upset, drunk and crazy tonight. I ain't got a clue what's going on."

"Okay, Speedy. I'll take care of this. We'll be fine." Speedy turned around and closed the door.

"So, you're the famous Jenny that Sam is so crazy about? You sure got a great body, and I must say the veil isn't bad. Call me Tony, by the way. Let's have a look." Jenny turned and walked slowly around the room, Tony's eyes admiring her. She spotted a bottle of gin and glasses on the bar.

"Go ahead, Jenny," Tony said. "Help yourself. That is, if Sam doesn't mind." Jenny poured a drink and gulped it down.

"Sam. Damn Sam. I don't belong to Sam. He's only staying with me to get off when he can't find any whores." She kept drinking and talking, in long spurts. Tony couldn't understand half of what she said. Several times, he had to catch her, to keep her from falling. Then finally he caught her, and they fell onto the couch.

Slowly, Jenny reached up and unbuttoned the three top buttons on her suit jacket and slipped it off.

"Now, wait just a minute, Jenny," Tony exclaimed. Jenny put her fingers on his lips and shushed him.

"Oh, don't worry, Tony. I do it for Sam all the time. Let me, Tony, pretty please." She unbuttoned his shirt and kissed his nipples.

Damn, she was good. He tried looking at her face through the veil. Then she lowered her head. Breathing in sharply, he completely surrendered himself to her. His pants were down. The rush of blood to his organ made him dizzy; it was a long-forgotten feeling, after Maria's death. Tony closed his eyes.

+++

The door opened and slammed shut. Sam stood in the doorway and didn't say a word.

Tony opened his eyes. "Great God Almighty, Sam! You could have knocked!" Tony quickly pulled his pants up.

Sam glared. "So, this is why you kept my ass in China so long, you son of a bitch!"

"Sam, now listen here. Nothing happened. I've never met Jenny before tonight."

"You Goddamn lying son of a bitch. She's just a girl! A drunk, stupid girl!"

Jenny watched as Sam reached for the 9mm Luger from his shoulder holster.

"Now, Sam, that's not necessary. Look, Sam, you're tired and you've been drinking. Let's talk about this. I'm Tony. You know how much I care about you. Jenny came to me. I swear I never would do this to you," Tony said, glancing at the door.

"Jenny, Jenny," Sam pleaded. "What have you done?"

Jenny shouted, "I'm through with you, Sam! I never want to see you again!"

Tony took a step toward Sam. Jenny stumbled and fell against Sam's arm. The blast silenced the room. Everybody stood still. Slowly, Jenny and Sam slid to the floor, holding each other. "I'm so sorry," Sam said.

She lay on top of Sam and whispered, "I know, Sam." The front of Jenny's yellow suit was covered in blood. Sam never heard her words.

Tony knelt next to Sam and checked for a heartbeat. He pulled Sam into his arms and sobbed.

Two bouncers who responded to the gunshot, pulled Jenny away.

CHAPTER ELEVEN

The Unknown

Anthony Salvadore struggled to be in charge, through the heartbreak of his childhood friend's death. He directed his words to Speedy, who had come in quickly after the gunshot. "Take Jenny down the back stairs to the house. Tell Clara to take care of her." He blew his nose. "The boys and I will take care of Sammy."

+++

Jenny choked in the back seat of Speedy's car. She was hysterical. The bouncers sat on each side of her.

"I need to go back! Sam needs me! Will he be okay?" She hit them with her fists, grabbed the door handle, and tried to jump out of the car. Eventually, the alcohol and exhaustion took over, and she fell into a stupor.

They arrived at Tony's house and gently blew the horn. A plump, older Negro woman opened the front door.

Benjamin, an elderly Negro man, followed her outside, looking over her shoulder at the car.

"Clara," Speedy said, "there's a woman in this car. There's been an accident. She's not hurt. That's somebody else's blood on her. Mr.

Salvadore said to take care of her. He'll see you tomorrow. We gotta get back now."

Clara stood watching the two big men pulling a little blood-soaked body from the back seat.

"Oh, Lord! Mr. Speedy, you say she ain't hurt? You sure?"

"Yes," replied Speedy, "she's drunk and upset. Mr. Salvadore wants you to take off those bloody clothes and give her something to help her sleep. Keep an eye on her. Get Benjamin to help you."

"Take her upstairs and put her in the bathroom," Clara instructed, "and you be quiet. Mr. Baxter is asleep at the end of the hall."

After placing Jenny on the bathroom floor, Speedy and the bouncers left.

Clara stared at the white girl. "Okay, honey, let old Clara get these clothes off." Jenny moaned, but was otherwise unaware. Clara removed the hair pins and the headband pinning the veil to her head, and slowly removed the veil.

"Good Jesus!" Clara crumbled to the floor and clutched her chest. "What in the name of the Lord...?" Clara looked at the unconscious Jenny. She moved slowly toward her and touched her hand. After a few minutes, Clara patted her. "All right, honey, it's all right."

Oh, Mr. Tony – what you gone and got yourself into? You and Mr. Sam gone too far this time. This is trouble. Trouble for all of us.

Clara finished Jenny's sponge bath and dressed her tiny frame in a pair of Baxter's pajamas. They were too big; after all, Baxter was twenty-one and weighed about 160 pounds. *That will have to do for tonight. Lord, I'm tired and too old for these kinds of doings.*

She hurried downstairs and found Benjamin sitting at the kitchen table. She touched him on the shoulder and he jumped. Clara thumped his cropped grey hair with an impatient huff.

"Clara, don't come up behind me like that. I'm old, and my heart is weak," Benjamin complained, rubbing his hand over his heart.

"Well," Clara said, lowering her voice. "When you see what I just saw upstairs, your heart may just stop altogether. Now, help me put that child to bed."

"Be quiet," she warned, before they entered the bathroom. "If you scream, I'm going to give you this." She touched Ben's nose with her fist.

"Clara," Benjamin said, "stop that! You always making mountains out of molehills."

Clara slowly opened the door, with Benjamin behind her. Jenny lay supine on the floor, her head toward the bathtub.

"Close the door, and don't make a sound," Clara ordered. She moved Jenny over to sit her up.

When Benjamin looked directly at Jenny's face, his legs collapsed under him.

"Clara, what is…? what is…?" Benjamin stammered.

Clara placed a finger on her lips to quiet him.

"I was afraid at first, but she's all right. Her face ain't all. Her whole *body* looks like one long railroad track… I guess they tried to put her back together, 'cause them are knife marks all over her. We got trouble now, Ben. We got a *mess* of trouble."

Together, they carried Jenny to the guest bedroom at the far end of the hall. It wasn't hard. She was light as a feather in their arms.

After they returned downstairs, Clara brewed a pot of strong coffee. "We got to keep a good eye on that child. Mr. Tony and Mr. Sam have a lot of explaining to do tomorrow. Lord, I'm tired.

You have a cup of this coffee and go upstairs, Ben. I'll wash these bloody clothes and get some breakfast ready. If Mr. Baxter asks, don't say a word. Let Mr. Tony tell him. After all, this is his daddy and Mr. Sam's doings."

Benjamin said. "I don't wanna go up there."

"Now, listen here," Clara snapped. "I can't be in two places at the same time. The Good Lord only saw fit to make one of me, so that leaves *you*, Ben. Anyway, she's already asleep. I gave her something. She'll sleep till she's sober, I pray."

+++

Anthony Salvadore had no interest in friends. Friends got you into trouble. Then, he met Sam. Both were sixteen years old and lived on the streets. Both had known hunger, women, and trouble. They got smart, or at least they thought they were smart, with a few bets here, two-bit break-ins there and then transporting stolen goods.

Tony and Sam had trusted each other and had each other's back at all times. Sam was best man at Tony's wedding, and godfather to Tony's only child, Baxter Samuel Salvadore. Sam stood beside Tony when Maria, Baxter's mother, died in childbirth. Tony would not have made it through those horrible days without him.

Now Sammy was lying dead in a pool of blood. Tony beat his chest and cried.

"Damn you, Sammy!" Tony cried out. "You went and fell in love! Why her? She's a drunk, a whore, a freak. She got you killed! Sammy, she took you from me. What'll I do now?" Tony wiped his eyes and blew his nose and watched Speedy and the boys drive up on the street below. Soon he heard a knock and opened the door.

"Oh, boss," Speedy said, "how could this happen? Tell me what to do!"

"Speedy," Tony said in a low voice, "can't you see? Sam *killed himself*, right here in front of me! When the cops get here, Speedy, don't forget you were standing right here and *saw everything*."

Following his boss's instructions, Speedy called the police station and requested the cops who patrolled the club area and were on Tony's payroll.

After questioning Tony for an hour, the cops took the gun from Sam's hand for fingerprint analysis, and a hearse took the body to the funeral home. There was no one to notify; Sam had no family. All his acquaintances would know by tomorrow.

Tony made all the funeral arrangements. *The only person I could ever trust.*

A meeting with the mob families was urgent. He told Speedy to arrange it before the wake, then told his driver to take him home.

Tony opened his front door and stepped inside. The huge house was quiet, but he heard a noise. He walked through the dining room and found Clara in the kitchen, washing dishes. He didn't want to surprise her, so he cleared his throat. Clara quickly turned around.

"Mr. Tony, glad you home. Breakfast's cooking."

Clara looked behind him, then walked over and looked into the dining room.

"Now, Mr. Tony, don't you and Mr. Sam play jokes on me. I had a busy night, thanks to you. When you get some food in you, I need some talking out of *both* of you. So, come on out, Mr. Sam, don't go fooling around this early in the morning. You two grown men acting like a couple of hot-headed boys."

"Clara," Tony said, sitting down at the kitchen table. "Sam's not here. Sammy's never coming here again."

"Aw, come on, Mr. Tony. You two been fighting again, but you always get back together. It might take a day or two, though. Mr. Sam's kinda stubborn."

Tony hit the table with his fists. Almost choking on the words, he said, "Sam is dead. He's *dead*, dammit, and that woman upstairs is responsible. Don't ask any questions. I'm going up to change clothes. Bring me some coffee." He stomped out, choking down a sob.

Clara held onto the back of the chair. *Oh, Lord, oh Lord, please help me.* She fixed the coffee, took it upstairs, put it on the dresser, and closed the door.

She hurried to the guest room and gently opened the door. Benjamin slept heavily in the chair; the girl was asleep in the bed.

That girl killed Mr. Sam. Mr. Tony never said killed, *said she was* responsible, *what does that mean?*

She leaned over and called softly, "Ben, Ben, wake up." He looked at Clara, who had tears in her eyes.

"Clara, what is it? You sick? What's the matter?"

"Ben, it's Mr. Sam. Mr. Sam is dead."

"What? How do you know that?"

Clara lowered her voice. "Mr. Tony came home. He's been in the kitchen, fussing and screaming, then he went to his room. I don't know any more, except…"

"Except what?" asked Benjamin.

"Except, oh, my Lord, Mr. Tony says *that girl* is responsible for Mr. Sam being dead.

Ben, I got to sit down. Go downstairs and eat. I need to be alone. I need to pray. Everything is going all wrong."

Benjamin stood and stretched his arms high over his head. He closed the door and shook his head. *Clara's tired; maybe she didn't hear it straight. Yeah, that's it. I'm sure of it.*

Benjamin ate breakfast and went into the garden. He planted the new rose bushes; the kind Miss Maria loved.

Mr. Tony's not the same since she died; he's all about business and money. Benjamin mulled on the thought about the girl upstairs as he worked. *Wonder what happened to her? There's gonna be trouble. Yes sir, trouble.*

Tony rushed downstairs and went out the front door before the tears started. Words couldn't express the deep hurt he felt. His driver stood beside the car. "Take me to the club, Charlie."

Clara came running out the house. "Mr. Tony, what about tonight's meal?"

"Just drive, Charlie," ordered Tony.

"Yes, sir," said the burly man who was Tony's combination driver and bodyguard.

Clara wiped her face with her apron, and went inside. All this had left her a bit dizzy.

+++

Jenny looked at the woman sitting in the chair and said, "Please help me."

Clara jumped out of the chair. The girl sat up and asked, "Where am I?"

Walking closer to the bed, *My Lord, what do I say? I'll just trust in Jesus, well here goes.*

"Honey, you're at Mr. Tony's house. They brought you here last night."

When Clara said those words, Jenny remembered one of the bouncers had said Sam was dead. She sobbed.

"Oh, Sam, I'm so sorry, Sam, please forgive me. My Sam's gone, and it's all my fault."

"You stay in that bed till Mr. Tony comes home," Clara said sternly.

"I don't care what he wants!" Jenny shouted. "*We killed Sam.* It was *his* fault, too."

"See here, you keep your voice down, young'un. Other people in this house still trying to sleep."

"Oh, I wish I'd never heard or seen Mr. Tony. I need a drink. I'll stay in this bed, but I'll damn well get drunk if I have to do it. So, bring it, or I'll go crazy."

"I'll get you something, if you promise to be quiet."

"You leave me alone," Jenny said. When she looked at Clara, there was fear in her eyes. "Where's my veil?"

"I washed it," Clara answered. "I'll get it and bring you something to calm down."

As Jenny lay back in bed, Clara heard her muttering, "I just want to die. Tony hates me. I hate me. I killed Sam."

+++

Clara fixed a breakfast tray and put a bottle of whiskey and the veil on it. *Let her drink until Mr. Tony can straighten out this mess.*

She pushed the kitchen door open, and Baxter walked in, wearing pajamas. The good-looking twenty-one-year old was a blond, blue-eyed reminder of his mother. He yawned and sat at the table.

"What you doing there, Clara?" Baxter asked, watching the full breakfast tray.

"Your breakfast is on the table, Mr. Baxter. I'm taking this to a guest your father brought home last night," Clara answered, gripping the tray.

"What in hell is that yellow thing on the tray?"

"That belongs to the guest. I washed it for her."

"'Her'? Our guest is a woman?" Baxter asked, looking a little more interested. "Could I have a peek, Clara?"

"No, sir, not until your father is back. Anyways, Mr. Charlie said when he gets back, Mr. Tony wants you to come down to the club."

"What? I'm not going there! I hate that place! They won't give me liquor, and I can't even sample the Chinese whores. No!" As usual, Baxter was agitated when he talked about the club.

"Now, Mr. Baxter, you quit talking like that. Something bad happened at the club. Mr. Tony said he needs you there this morning. Mr. Charlie will be back in an hour, so eat and get dressed. Don't upset Mr. Tony any more than he already is."

"Well," Baxter said as he started breakfast, "when I get back, I want to meet our guest."

+++

The mob family gathered at the club in the large upstairs room. Charlie walked in with Baxter.

Tony sat in his chair at one end of the large conference table. The chair at the other end remained empty. Baxter went over to sit in it.

"Don't sit in that chair, now or ever, Baxter!" Tony shouted. Everyone except Baxter knew Sam always sat in that chair. Baxter, stunned at his father's outburst, leaned against the wall.

"Gentlemen, if you don't already know, I'll tell you." Anthony Salvadore spoke slowly and carefully. "Sam is dead. He shot himself last night." There was a startled burst of talk around the table.

"What? Shit!" Baxter screamed. He bowed his head and pounded his fists on his thighs. "Last week, Sam promised we could spend a whole day, just the two of us, on a drive up the coast. Why would he promise me that and then go and shoot himself? It doesn't make sense!"

A moment later, Tony spoke, but Baxter, distraught, didn't answer. "Baxter, answer the question!"

"What question?" Baxter closed his eyes, trying to process the information.

"Mr. Salvadore," Speedy said, "the boy's in shock." He repeated for Tony. "Baxter, your dad asked you to give Sam's eulogy. Can you do it?"

Baxter shook his head vigorously. "What? No way! I'm getting out of here. Sam didn't shoot himself. I *know* he wouldn't do that. Not Sammy. He loved living. He was happy. You're all lying. I know it. You know what really happened. I'm leaving. I *hate* this place!"

As he turned to leave, he knocked the empty chair over. Tony bounded out his chair and pointed a finger at Baxter. Speedy quickly put his hand on Tony's shoulder.

"Mr. Salvadore," he said warmly. "Go on, you finish the plans. I'll see about him."

Tony sat down. Speedy followed Baxter.

"Hold up there," Speedy called. He grabbed Baxter's arm. "Have a smoke."

He lit two cigarettes, offered one to Baxter. Together, they went slowly downstairs. He led Baxter into a booth. Speedy noticed the club was empty.

"Have you seen Sam these last few weeks?" Speedy asked.

"No," Baxter answered. "If anything went wrong, it's a problem with the China deals. Sam wouldn't shoot himself. He just *wouldn't*."

"Well," Speedy said, "you don't know everything about Sam's life. You take my word that a woman was involved."

"Sam was involved with a lot of women."

"No," Speedy continued. "This one was different. Sam cared about her, but she was nothing but trouble. Driving him crazy with her drinking, threatening to leave him. Your dad sent him to China to give him a chance to sort things out. He wanted to get rid of her before Sam came back. I think she found out and tried to blackmail or double-cross them. Sam just couldn't take it anymore. I think he actually loved her."

"Did my father find Sam, I mean, after Sam had done it?"

"Your dad heard voices shouting upstairs, coming from his office. The woman and Sam were arguing. Your dad started up the stairs and heard a gunshot. I went up and found him on the floor holding Sam in his arms. The woman sat on the floor crying. She was drunk. Naturally."

"Damn her to hell!" Baxter said. He smashed a glass against the wall. The bartender looked up. Speedy motioned him to let it be. He got another beer for Baxter.

"Tell my dad I'll go to the funeral, but I cannot say Sam's eulogy. I just can't, Speedy." Baxter had tears in his eyes. Speedy helped Baxter into the waiting car, leaned over and whispered to the bodyguard, "Charlie, Mr. Salvadore will be down shortly. Just let Baxter sit here and wait."

Baxter sat in the car and cried, while Charlie kept his back turned. After an hour, Baxter blew his nose and fell asleep in the back seat. The booze was taking effect, especially with what Speedy had put in it.

+++

For the next two days, Jenny ate little of the food Clara brought her. She knew she was being drugged, but she didn't care; either she slept or she'd go crazy.

I've caused the death of a good friend, and now I'm in his best friend's house. And to make it worse, I'm still alive.

After Clara's last visit to Jenny's room, Jenny walked to the bathroom, and poured the contents into the sink.

While taking a bath, she started thinking. *I need to know more about Tony. My drinking days are over, and my learning days are starting. What is he telling everyone? I have to be careful; Tony's a violent man.*

She put on her suit. *I hate wearing this, even with the blood washed out, but I don't have a choice.* She put her veil over her face, with pins and her headband, took a deep breath and slowly descended the stairs. Immediately, she entered into the most beautiful room Jenny had ever seen. There was a giant chandelier with hundreds of crystal teardrop lights, a marble floor, wraparound fireplace and a white piano in the corner. She wandered outside, unable to believe such splendid beauty.

The endless yard reached the imposing iron entrance gate. Next to the gate, bloomed an enormous rose garden, creating the fragrance of hidden pleasures.

She strolled over to enjoy the view and noticed an elderly Negro man on his knees, digging in the garden.

As she approached, he stood and brushed some of the dirt off the knees of his pants.

"Hello," Jenny said.

Benjamin said nothing. She kept talking.

"My name's Jenny Stone. I guess I'm staying here for now."

"Mr. Tony's not here," Benjamin blurted out.

"I know," Jenny said. "There's no one home."

"Yes, ma'am, Clara be in the kitchen. She's always home."

"Those roses are breathtaking. What did you say your name is?"

"Benjamin, Miss."

"Well, hello, Mr. Benjamin." Jenny turned and gazed at the beautiful mansion that seemed to float on its green lawns.

She heard the Negro man mutter, "*Mr. Benjamin*, now *that* is something to tell old Clara. Yes, sir, *Mr.* Benjamin."

Jenny continued toward the door, as a car came up the driveway. The back door opened, and Tony and a young man stepped out.

"Dad, who is that woman?" Baxter whispered.

"A friend of Sam's. She's staying till the funeral. Charlie, take Baxter inside." Tony walked slowly to Jenny.

"Well, you're doing better than I thought. Over Sam so quickly?" he said sarcastically. "I thought I knew him, but I guess I was wrong. What's with the veil? Sam told me you had an accident. Do you wear that all the time? Just how bad are you?"

"That's none of your damn business, Tony. I don't need to explain anything to you," Jenny said.

"Now, Jenny, calm down and listen. I don't believe you want to get involved with the cops any more than I do. Things are complicated."

"What do you mean? It was an accident," Jenny stammered.

"Yeah, we know. I owe you for saving my life," Tony answered. "The cops didn't want a sad story. I told them Sam started drinking, appeared depressed and moody, with unexplained explosive behavior. Sam seemed troubled. He was out of his head when he did it."

"Tony, how could you say such a thing? Everybody knows Sam wouldn't take his own life. No one would believe that, not for a second," Jenny said, looking directly into Tony's eyes.

Tony's muscles tightened beneath his shirt. "We said Speedy and I tried to stop him. Sam became upset and irrational. It happened fast. End of story."

He pointed a finger at Jenny. "I got a son whose mother died in childbirth, and now his godfather is dead. Baxter loved Sammy more than me. He was more of a father to my son than I could be. So, I did what I had to do. Now, you can stay here and cause no trouble. Like I said, I owe you. If you even breathe *one word* of what went on in that room, Jenny, I will make your life a living hell. Don't ever push me. I am not Sam, and whatever you had on him will not work on me. No woman is worth dying over. Sammy proved that."

Jenny gripped the sides of her head in anguish. "No, no, no. Everyone will think Sam committed suicide. My God, I can't!"

"You can, and you will," Tony threatened. He marched into the house.

Jenny knew in her heart she would keep this secret. She had no choice. Her life had become a series of secrets. *At least there's comfort knowing you're safe, my son, my darling Jet.*

Chapter Twelve

The Announcement

From Sam's graveside, Jenny saw Baxter's eyes glaring at her. Wherever she turned, there were his eyes.

+++

Afterward, she checked around corners, avoiding Baxter. He stayed with friends for several days after the funeral.

Jenny occupied her time working in the garden, re-playing past events; she was unable to concentrate on anything else.

She hated to ask Tony, but she needed clothes. *Damn, I hate to ask him for a red cent, but I have no choice.*

When she finally worked up the courage to ask, he just grunted and motioned her to leave. The following evening, Clara came to her bedroom with a stack of dresses, then carefully separated the material and hand-stitched each dress to fit Jenny's emaciated figure. No cash was included.

Jenny began to follow Clara around. "Have you ever been married?" she asked one day.

"No. Clara explained. "Left the South when I was about twenty-four. Met Ben running too. We found our way to Back Road. There was utter poverty outside of Back Road. Mr. Tony said he would not own a Negro ghetto, so he kept everyone working and our town had hope. Nobody mess with the people from Back Road. Me and Ben started working for Miss Maria. She had that little cottage built for us. That child wasn't happy, but she had a lot of love inside. This became my home, and I asked no questions." Jenny thought it was very good for her that she hadn't.

+++

Jenny stayed away from Sam's apartment and kept out of Baxter's way. Baxter stayed out late and then slept all day.

"Truth be told," Clara told Jenny, "Baxter and his white friends hang out at the Negro Back Road Club. It's not his fault," Clara continued. "That boy lives with lots of heartache and grief. He was alone, most of the time, except for Mr. Sam. Lost his mother and now, Mr. Sam."

According to Clara, Baxter was aware of Jenny's involvement with Sam, but not the real story, just Tony's version. She suspected Tony's version made her sound irresponsible and selfish.

Early one Sunday morning, Jenny put on a dignified little red dress, white pumps, a white bowl hat with a white veil and bounced down the stairs to the kitchen.

"Hello, Momma Clara." Clara loved hearing those words, and quickly turned from the stove.

"Well, look at you, Jenny girl. What you up to this early?"

Jenny smiled, sat down, and announced, "I'm going to church with you and Benjamin."

"Oh, no, you ain't," came the immediate reply. Clara turned her back, so Jenny would not see her smiling.

"Oh, but I am. You told me God would help me. You said that God is in that little church, so that's where I'll be today."

"Now Jenny," said Clara anxiously. She knew Jenny was serious. "There's only Negro folks there, and I mean, what will Mr. Tony think?"

"I don't see a Mr. Tony," Jenny said mischievously. "I won't tell him, but you can if you want."

As the two women starred at each other, Benjamin came in, dressed in his Sunday suit.

"Well, Miss Jenny, don't you look like a picture. Going somewhere?"

"Yes, sir, I'm going to church with you and Momma Clara."

"You *what*?" stuttered Benjamin. "Clara Mae, what you gone and done?"

"I ain't done nothing and she ain't going," announced Clara.

"Please, Mr. Benjamin." Jenny pretended she was about to cry. "I don't want to be here all day with Baxter upstairs drunk. Please?"

Clara threw her hands up in the air. "Well, there'll be trouble now."

Jenny jumped up and threw both arms around Clara. "I promise to be quiet."

When Jenny entered the church, there was silence.

The service began with several songs. Soon, it was obvious to Clara, Benjamin and the congregation that Jenny had a beautiful singing voice. Jenny closed her eyes, tipped her head back, and let the moment take her away. She didn't realize everyone else was quiet. She sang *Amazing Grace* alone.

When she stopped, the preacher and the entire congregation shouted, "Amen!"

Walking home, Clara had never been so happy. *If I had a daughter, I would want her to be Jenny.*

109

"Momma Clara, I'm starving. Is church always so long? Next time I'll eat a big breakfast or pack some food," Jenny said.

"You better be hungry. And tonight, apple and peach pie: That's Mr. Tony's and Mr. Baxter's favorite. I also fixed chicken and dumplings, cornbread, black-eyed peas, and my special red cabbage slaw."

After they ate and cleaned up, Clara asked, "Jenny, where'd you learn to sing like that? Honey, it was beautiful. I know that voice of yours went straight to heaven."

"A very long time ago, I sang along with my special friend, Maggie. She knew all the songs," Jenny answered.

Clara watched Jenny's face turn from hope to despair. She quickly changed the subject.

"Jenny, today I want you to try on a suit I been working on. I think it will look just fine for next Sunday."

"What," exclaimed Jenny, "you mean that I can go back with you and Benjamin?"

"Oh, child, everyone wants you back," soothed Clara.

+++

On a hot July night, Jenny sat in her room. Baxter and his friends were especially loud tonight. They were spoiled brats who had become angry young men.

In a moment of quiet, she heard them talking about The Back Road Club, where they went often. The front door closed, and she heard Baxter's car leaving the driveway.

The club was in the Negro section of town. Tony's splendid mansion displayed its beauty on top of the hillside separated from Back Road by an oak forest. Sometimes, with the window open, she could faintly hear the music. Tonight, she decided she would go there, as well. It was time to be with other people, for a change.

Jenny put on her red dress, veil and white lace gloves. Nervously, in the darkness, she hiked down the long, dirt road and saw the club, which had at least twenty cars parked on the dirt lot. The jazz and blues music rang loud and exciting.

She peeked inside. The place was smoky and crowded. Everyone was laughing and having a good time. In the audience, she saw Baxter and his friends, drunk and loud. Several white men danced with Negro girls.

Jenny stood and listened to two male coronet and trombone players performed, then a piano player. She knew the words to every song. Wanting to hear more, she went to the back door, where an elderly man tipped his hat and opened the door for her. She went inside and stood in a dark corner, where she could not be seen by Baxter.

"Now, don't be shy," a male voice said. It was so unexpected, Jenny had to cover her mouth to keep from screaming. He went on. "When that guy finishes, you're on next. The piano player will follow whatever song you choose. You sure don't look like a jazz and blues singer, but if they want you back, we'll discuss a little pay."

"Oh! No," Jenny said. "That's not me."

He wasn't listening; he was already onstage introducing Jenny as the Red Siren.

Oh, what the hell? Baxter's drunk. He's never seen me dressed up. I might get away with it.

She swallowed a laugh, thinking about her introduction,and stepped onto the stage. Peering into the crowd, she was delighted to see Baxter was leaving.

Jenny walked over to the microphone and began to sing an old Louis Armstrong favorite, *A Kiss to Build a Dream On*. The piano came in easily behind her, and she keep on singing, putting her heart into it, forgetting for a moment the nightmares and the hurt. She kept singing about that special someone.

Everyone applauded as Jenny left the stage and started out. The manager stopped her.

"Just a minute, Red Siren, somebody wants to meet you. Hope you liked your introduction; we don't care for names here."

"No, I can't. I have to go." Jenny tried to get past the man. Then she heard a female voice.

"Hello." The woman's full lips glowed a vibrant red. She wore a green jeweled dress over her golden tan skin. "Before you go, let me introduce myself. I'm Ruby." She extended her hand in a genuine gesture of friendship. "I own this club. Now, who are you? I know you're not the girl who was supposed to be here."

"I just came in to hear the music," Jenny explained. "Before I knew it, I was told to sing. I apologize."

"Well," Ruby said, "you sing like a songbird. What did you say your name is?"

"Jenny."

"Jenny, if you come back Saturday night, you can put out a tip jar. Everything in it will be yours," she explained. "We can talk about wages after your next performance. Do you live near here?"

Jenny thought for a minute. "I'm staying at Mr. Salvadore's until I find my own place."

"Well, good. But there's one thing," Ruby said. "You don't *have* to wear that veil, do you? Are you hiding from someone?"

Jenny turned and left, saying, "Thanks, Miss Ruby."

"Now," Ruby said, "that girl is classy. Sonny," she ordered, "don't let those drunk white boys back in my place tonight."

+++

Jenny, Clara, and Benjamin became a little family of churchgoers. Clara encouraged Jenny to sing during services. She smiled and looked as proud as any Momma, when Jenny sang Clara's favorite hymn, *Amazing Grace.*

Afterward, Clara and Benjamin talked about her.

"When that child sings my song, it sounds like an angel," Clara said.

"Well," Benjamin replied, "if Mr. Tony finds out, our lives will be hell."

"You watch your mouth, Benjamin Cook. Who's going to tell him? Not my baby girl. Poor Mr. Baxter, he don't know one day from the next, and Sunday means nothing to him. He's headed for a heap of trouble, and all his money won't save him."

+++

Clara didn't know Jenny went to The Back Road Club almost every Saturday night. Jenny never drank or socialized; she went there to sing.

And sing she did. The audiences loved her. With her tips and the extra wages from Ruby, her savings began to create some independence toward a new beginning.

She asked Ruby to buy her some clothes to wear at the club for her performances. She always left the clothes in the club's dressing room after she sang.

Ruby knew Jenny's face was disfigured. Once, she entered the dressing room to leave clothes. Jenny was unaware of her presence, and her veil was off.

Ruby saw the old scars in the dressing-table mirror. She knew those scars hadn't happened recently, but she also decided Jenny's past was none of her business, and the veil gave a seductive feel to

Jenny's performance. Ruby selected material for each veil to match Jenny's outfits.

Jenny didn't sing every Saturday; she sneaked out once or twice a month, always waiting until Clara went to bed. She longed to tell Momma Clara, but this was something she wouldn't understand. Jenny had to keep this a secret. She needed the money, which was her first step toward freedom. Her club family accepted her without question.

Jenny promised Sonny she would perform with the band on Ruby's birthday. In the past year, her little family had come to include Ruby, Ruby's boyfriend Solomon, Sonny, the bouncer, and the guys in the band. There was nothing she wouldn't do for them.

Jenny waited patiently until Clara went to bed, then hurried out the back door, ran to the club, and changed into her new red dress, the only color that Jenny would let Ruby buy for her. The collar and cuffs were rich black velvet with rhinestones and simulated pearls, and the dress was cut in a low V-neck, with netting that covered her bare skin and a high black waist band. Silver t-strap high heels finished the outfit. Ruby had lent her a beautiful pearl necklace and left a veil with matching red netting attached to a satin headband on Jenny's dressing table.

The club had been turned into a ballroom, with green ceiling lights on the ceiling, balloons with green streamers and Happy Birthday signs. Green was Ruby's good-luck color.

Sonny announced, "The Red Siren!" There was shouting and clapping. Ruby leaned against the bar with Solomon. Jenny stood at the microphone. "Tonight, I'll sing a special song for my friend, Miss Ruby Benson." The band started to play *Everywhere You Go,* the song made famous by Guy Lombardo and his Royal Canadians. Ruby closed her eyes and leaned against Solomon's chest.

After the applause, Sonny brought out the cake, and Jenny led everyone in singing *Happy Birthday.* Several friends insisted Ruby and Solomon dance a birthday dance. The band began playing *Saint Louis Blues,* a simple swing dance, and the two took the floor. Everyone joined in, even Jenny.

It was getting late when Jenny saw Baxter and his friends walk in.

She quickly left the floor and went to the back room, where she changed clothes.

There was a knock. Ruby staggered in, put her arms around Jenny and gave her a hug.

"Why, Miss Ruby," Jenny teased. "I do believe you've been drinking."

"This is my best birthday ever," Ruby said. "Don't go yet. Sonny is throwing those loud-mouth drunk white boys out. We'll lock the door and really party."

"I can't. You know Momma Clara. She'll kill me." Jenny listened to the band, and danced alone in the dressing room to the *Jazz Band Ball* before leaving to walk home. Ruby's hug made her feel she mattered.

What a beautiful night, warm and breezy with a full moon. She thought about removing the veil and letting the wind blow her hair, but wasn't aware of the approaching car until the lights were shining on her.

As the car approached, she recognized the loud voices of Baxter and his friends. The car slowed beside her. Baxter yelled, "Get in the damn car!"

Jenny walked faster. They sped up. She ran.

"Don't be a 'fraidy cat, come on, get in." The car door opened. One of the boys grabbed her arm to pull her into the car. She reached up with the other hand and dug her nails into his flesh. He let go. She slid down an embankment and fell into a ditch. They stopped the car and got out. Terrified, she stayed quiet.

"Aw, come on," one of the guys said. "Come on, Baxter. I feel sick. Let's go."

"Damn it," Baxter pouted. "I wanted to have some fun with the bitch that made Uncle Sammy die."

Jenny heard feet on asphalt and doors open and closing. Mercifully, the car drove away.

Well, that was close. From now on, I'll have Sonny bring me home. Her heart beat so hard, it hurt her ears.

The next day she didn't say a word to Clara or Benjamin about the incident with Baxter. Jenny knew she must hasten her plans to leave. She loved the club, church, Momma Clara and Benjamin, but her time to live there was running out. *I need to save more money. Ruby could help me find a place nearby. I* must *get out of here.*

+++

One morning in late November, Benjamin drove Clara and Jenny to the Negro community to see a young girl who had a baby boy. Clara was teaching her to care for the infant. Jenny helped; it felt so good to hold a baby again. Every inch of her body cuddled the baby. Memories of Jet unleashed tears.

"What's wrong, honey?" Momma Clara asked. The look on Jenny's face answered the question. Momma Clara put her arms around Jenny and let her cry.

The next morning, Jenny declined to go to town with Clara.

Clara said, "Well, then, I left something on the stove you can eat. Jenny, you starting to lose weight again. I think it's all that walking you been doing. Next time you want to visit your town friends, ask Ben to take you."

Jenny waved goodbye, went upstairs and opened her dresser drawer to count her savings. She heard the car come back. Momma Clara had forgotten her grocery list, again. She looked out the window to tell her she'd bring it to her and saw Baxter and his three buddies.

They drank booze, ate the leftovers in the refrigerator and went upstairs to Baxter's room.

Jenny decided they were likely to stay there for awhile, if they didn't pass out. Now she should see Ruby about getting a place of her own and maybe even tell her about Jet. Ruby would never judge or question. She went quietly to the top of the stairs.

Baxter's door opened, and out they came.

"Well, well," Baxter said. "Look who we have here. Cleopatra, the whore." They all laughed. She started to walk downstairs, but Baxter grabbed her arm. "Before you go, I need a little favor."

Jenny thought of how he swaggered around the house, drank constantly and lorded it over everyone. Just thinking of it after all these months enraged her. She turned on him. "Now let me tell *you* something, you son of a bitch. You and your friends need to grow up and learn some manners. You think you know everything, you're too damn stupid to know anything."

Baxter was taken by surprise; Jenny had hardly spoken to him since she arrived. When her words sank in, he hit her across the mouth, grabbed her arm, and yelled for the others to help him. They pulled her to his room, with Jenny struggling all the way.

They threw her on the floor, and Baxter unzipped his pants.

With his drunken breath close to her face, he shouted to the others, "Now, let's see what's under this veil, and then we'll find out what's under the dress." Still laughing, he leaned down and tore her veil off.

117

She heard an awful gasp as they saw her bare face. "God Almighty!" Baxter said. "What the hell? What are you?" He jumped up and kicked Jenny. "Get away from me. You are one ugly bitch."

Baxter paced across the room. He didn't seem to know what to do. He wouldn't look at Jenny. "Fucking whore!" he shouted, remembering his father's snide comments about Sam's death. After all this time, he *still* couldn't put the puzzle pieces together!

Furious all over again at what he still couldn't understand, he turned to his buddies. "Help me put her in the closet."

They pulled her across the floor to the closet. Jenny fought furiously, but they held her arms, so she kicked and screamed. They pushed her inside and closed the door. She pounded on the door and kept screaming.

Baxter looked at his pet snake in its glass cage. It wasn't enough just to lock her in; he wanted to do something else.

He opened the lid of the cage, grabbed the snake behind the head and picked up the body with his other hand. His once-interesting plaything had become too docile, unless he poked it with a stick. He put the snake through the space beneath the closet door.

The tall boy said, "Baxter, does that snake bite?"

"Nah, he's not hungry. I fed him before I left. And he's not poisonous, but it'll scare the hell out of her. All the freak has to do is open the damn door to get out."

They walked out of the bedroom.

"Go ahead, I forgot my jacket." Baxter returned to his room, took out a key, locked the closet door, shook it violently and whispered, "That's for Sam."

Jenny sat in the dark closet. The light switch was outside the door. *I underestimated his hatred of me.* As soon as I can get out of here, I'm leaving this house.

Her thoughts were interrupted by something moving. She screamed out loud. *Oh God, a mouse just bit me on the ankle!* She reached down; something bit her on the hand. It felt like a pair of needles going into her flesh.

She moved closer to the door, twisting the handle, trying to push her way out. Then the thing bit her leg.

Be still. Stay calm. She held her arms tight to her body. The thing bit her on the leg again. She reached down, felt a long, warm scaly thing and screamed!

Needles pricked her hand again. Provoked and angry, the snake had nowhere to retreat. He bit each time Jenny attacked.

Nausea and panic took over. She took her shoe off and hit anywhere and everywhere, but the sharp pains kept coming. She tried desperately to kick the door open. With each bite of the snake, she grew weaker.

Finally, the snake retreated to a corner. *Now, it is surely over.* Darkness and fear took her quietly away.

+++

Clara and Ben stacked supplies in the kitchen cupboard, wondering where Jenny was. Clara sent Ben to the rose garden, but he reported on returning that she wasn't there.

"I'm going upstairs," Clara declared. "If Mr. Baxter is sleeping off a drunk, I'll teach that boy a thing or two."

She marched upstairs and knocked on Baxter's door. "You get yourself up, Mr. Baxter, or I'm coming in." She waited a minute, pacing the hall. "Okay, I warned you." She went into the room and saw the mess Baxter and his friends had left.

What in the name of heaven? Jenny's veil lay, torn, by the closet. Clara tried to open the closet door. It was locked. She switched on the light and got no response from inside.

She went to the top of the stairs and screamed, "Ben, Ben, bring a hammer and get up here! Something is bad wrong!"

Ben ran in, hammer in hand, and hit at the doorknob until it broke. The door opened. Jenny's unconscious form fell out.

Clara screamed and cried. Ben saw Baxter's snake on the other side of Jenny's body. With the hammer, he hit it with powerful blows, until the snake stopped moving.

Clara kept crying. "Ben, call Dr. Stevens and tell him about the snake. Tell him to hurry, Ben. Is my baby alive?" She held Jenny's head and shoulders, cried and hugged her. Clara couldn't think what else to do.

Ben came back in. "Dr. Stevens said, put cold towels on her, put pillows under her head. Clara, is she breathing?"

"Oh, Jesus, my baby. Oh, baby girl, don't you leave your Momma Clara now," she prayed.

"Clara," Ben said sternly, "is she breathing?"

"What?" Clara looked dazed. "Yes, yes, Ben, she is."

"Then come on!" Ben ordered. "Let's do what the doctor said."

They undressed her, cleaned all the bites that they saw, and were putting towels over her when Dr. Stevens yelled from downstairs. "Up here!" Ben yelled back.

+++

Dr. Stevens had known Tony and his family for a long time, and had delivered Baxter.

He knew about Baxter's problems. Sam had talked to him about getting Baxter away from this house and his drinking friends. He'd heard about Sam's disfigured girlfriend, and how she remained with Tony after Sam's death.

+++

Dr. Stevens entered the room. Clara was crying, kneeling by the towel-covered body. Ben stood nearby, wringing his hands.

The doctor immediately noticed the disfigurement of the young woman's body. "Clara, let me take a look." *Dear God, at least five snake bites.*

"Is that the snake?"

"Yes," Clara answered. "It was Baxter's pet."

"All right. I'll give her the anti-venom and a tetanus shot, just in case. The bites aren't deep. I don't see any teeth fragments, but there are seven that I can count. She'll be very sick for at least a week from the bites. The snake probably did not release venom. The dry bites are a defense mechanism, and in this case, it wouldn't waste the venom on her. I'll leave her here for now. She's small; I think that's why she's unconscious. Now, would somebody tell me what happened?"

"We don't know," Clara answered. "We got home from town and found her locked in the closet. We think Mr. Baxter and his friends did it."

"Why do you say that?"

"Because he hates Jenny. He thinks she caused Mr. Sam's death. Mr. Baxter is all mixed up, with his drinking and crazy talk. I know he and his friends were in this house and did this to my baby."

"Where's Tony?" Dr. Stevens asked.

"We don't know that, either," Ben answered. "He left about a month ago, on business. We don't know about his doings, and that's for the best. There's trouble here," he said darkly. "Lots of trouble."

"I'm leaving this medicine, Clara," Dr. Stevens instructed. "Let her sleep about three hours, wake her up and give her a dose. She'll be in a lot of pain.

Keep the towels on her face and arms, no tight clothing. Put the antibiotic ointment on the bite marks. If she has any distress, call me at once. In the meantime, I'll find Tony Salvadore. Baxter's behavior has to end. Whether Tony likes it or not, his son needs a father. I'll be back tomorrow.

Ben, hold this bag open. I need to confirm the kind of snake for future treatment."

After Dr. Stevens left, Jenny lay in Baxter's bed, half conscious, with feverish nightmares, talking out of her head about Jet, nurses, and an angel. Sometimes, she just screamed, like she was being killed. Clara would rush over and hold her until she calmed down. After several days, the chills and fever were gone. The snake bites were still visible. She remained weak. Her throat was swollen from all the screaming for help, but she could sit on the side of the bed. Clara spent long hours praying and singing over her.

No one heard from Baxter. Dr. Stevens visited often. He sent a message to Tony, who was in China and expected home on Saturday.

True to his word, Saturday at 10:00 a.m., Dr. Stevens drove up the driveway. Ten minutes later, a car pulled up and Tony's driver opened the door. Tony and Baxter got out.

Clara was upstairs with Jenny.

There was a knock on the bedroom door. "Come in," Clara said. She was surprised to see Baxter and Dr. Stevens.

Tony looked around. "This is a family meeting," he said gruffly. "Everyone here gives straight answers. I need facts, is that clear?" All nodded, including Baxter, who never looked up.

As the story unfolded, Baxter sulkily admitted he and his friends forced Jenny into the closet, tossed the snake in and locked the door.

During all the talk, Jenny fell asleep.

Tony dismissed everyone except Doctor Stevens. "What's on your mind, Tom?" Tony asked.

"Tony, we've known each other a long time. We've both seen some awful things. Let me show you what this girl has endured." Dr. Stevens pulled the covers back. There were red ugly bitemarks on her arms, legs, and under the veil. Then Dr. Stevens showed Tony the stab and graft wounds from Jenny's past experience. "Tony, Sam knew something about this and still loved this girl. You and I and the girl know what happened to Sam."

"Shut up, Tom," Tony said. "My best friend tried to kill me. Now, my son did this. Correction: Sam's son. Oh, yes, I've always known it. Now, he's becoming more and more like me. Get out, Tom. Leave me the hell alone."

Dr. Stevens hesitated. *My God, how did Tony find out?* He shook his head and left. Tony sat down beside the bed. He reached out and took Jenny's frail hand.

"I'm sorry, Jenny. I think we're two of a kind. From now on, I'll be here for you, and you can be here for me." But Jenny was asleep and never heard his words.

+++

Weeks, months passed. The household slid into the quicksand of depression. Jenny remained determined to fulfill her plan to leave. Baxter was sullen, angry, and grew more and more uncomfortable around his father.

For three hours on a Saturday evening, the two of them exchanged such harsh words that Jenny, Benjamin, and Clara left the house and drove to the old cemetery behind the church to visit Maria and Sam's gravesites.

CHAPTER THIRTEEN

The Forgiving

Friday, May 22, 1943 haunted the people in the mansion for years. A black car with a seal printed on its side pulled onto the driveway. A man in a military uniform emerged, carrying a briefcase. Jenny hurried downstairs.

Benjamin welcome the man and escorted him to Tony's library. Within minutes, Jenny saw Baxter enter the library. Jenny hurried to the kitchen.

Clara was preparing a tray of sandwiches, fruit, and drinks. "What's going on?" Jenny asked.

"Well," Clara wiped her hands on her apron. "It looks like Mr. Tony put Mr.Baxter in the Army."

"What! When did this happen?"

Clara continued. "Mr. Tony called the army recruiter. Mr. Baxter ain't got a choice. He's going to serve his country. Mr. Tony told him, if he did his three years in the army, there'll be a bank account with his name on it. Let me tell you, I don't care what that boy does, as long as it's far away from here!"

Three days later, Clara, Jenny and Benjamin watched Tony and Baxter get into the black car with the seal on the side.

+++

As the months passed, Clara taught Jenny to sew. Benjamin showed her how to care for the roses. Jenny no longer went to The Back Road Club. Tony kept his word. She bought whatever she needed. He paid without asking questions. She did not have an income, however. She ordered and studied books about business record-keeping while sitting in the cozy sunroom. Most of all, she enjoyed going with Momma Clara to see the newborns in the Negro part of town.

The first week of December, Tony received a letter from Baxter, saying he'd be coming home for Christmas. Although no one wanted the disturbances Baxter brought to the house, everyone was getting in the holiday spirit.

Jenny and Clara decorated the house. Benjamin put up a beautiful tree. They planned a huge and festive party.

Two days before Christmas, Tony told everyone that Baxter would be arriving that afternoon. He would meet him at the train station.

Jenny watched out the upstairs window. As they got out of the car, Tony and Baxter both laughed, trying to carry Baxter's luggage. Jenny stared. Baxter looked impressive in his uniform, with a confident walk and straight, broad shoulders. She could almost imagine Baxter was happy.

Jenny went to her room, to keep from interrupting the reunion, and fell asleep on the bed.

Two hours later, a noise woke her. Someone was sitting beside the bed. She jerked up and almost screamed. It was Baxter.

125

"What are you doing here? Get out! There are people in the house, and I have a big voice when I want it heard."

Baxter smiled. "Hold on, Jenny. I came in to leave this for you. I saw you sleeping and thought I might sit here for a while."

Jenny felt her heart thumping. "Baxter," she said anxiously, "what do you want?"

"Nothing, I swear, Jenny. Here's your Christmas present. You can open it tomorrow, if you want." She looked at him. He was looking at her hopefully, holding out a small, blue, beautifully-wrapped box.

Her hand shook as she remembered the threats Baxter hurled at her that horrible day, but Jenny finally took the box.

"Jenny," he continued. "The army changed my life. I still have a lot to learn, but I'll never give up. When I return to my platoon, I'll take charge of the map squads, detailing logistical routes the infantry camp will take into Germany. This is something that I am good at. I put all my energy into the details, for the safety of our troops. You see, now I'm thinking of others, and it's a good feeling."

"Baxter—" Jenny interrupted.

"No, wait." He held up his hands. "Jenny, I was one hell of a mixed-up kid. I did some dumb, dangerous, awful things. I regret them. My father told me about you and Sam, said the shooting was a crazy accident, and you tried to stop it. I want to apologize for all the mean, hurtful things I did to you. I've seen what men look like after battles. I don't know what happened to you, but I do know you went through your own war. Please, let's be friends, if you can forgive me."

Jenny did not say a word.

"Well," Baxter said, "I know it's a lot to ask. Think about it." He got up and left the room and he seemed, as Jenny watched him leave, as though a heavy weight had fallen off his shoulders.

Clara and Benjamin had worked non-stop on the party preparations. Jenny hurried into the kitchen for a turkey sandwich.

She couldn't remember the last time the house had smelled so good. Benjamin had a roaring fire in the large marble fireplace. Clara had prepared pies, cakes, puddings, and enough food for an army. Just before the quests arrived, Benjamin placed roses throughout the house. Every room had a special bouquet.

"Lord, thank you, Jesus," Clara said. "This is the best Christmas since Miss Maria was alive. It's about time, too."

Tony seemed the perfect host. When he talked about Baxter, one saw *proud* all over his face. Several times, he put his arm around Baxter's shoulders or whispered something in Baxter's ear, which made both men laugh.

When they were about to eat, Baxter looked for Jenny and didn't see her, so he went upstairs. Her bedroom door was open. Baxter tried to speak when he saw her, but no sound came out.

"Now, listen, I need a favor," Jenny said. "Before we eat, you introduce me as Jenny Stone, a friend and singer. I have something planned for your father." She told him, as they went downstairs. He noticed she was wearing his gift, a tiny gold cross necklace.

Tony almost dropped his wine glass when they appeared on the stairs. There was Baxter, in his tuxedo and gleaming blond hair and Jenny, in her beautiful red dress with matching veil, and black curls that took his breath away.

At the bottom of the staircase, Baxter said, "Friends, we have a surprise and a treat for you before dinner. Miss Jenny Stone, a family friend and singer, will bring in the holiday season with a special song, *When You Wish Upon a Star,* accompanied by Doctor Stevens on the piano."

Baxter whispered in Jenny's ear, "You got this," and stepped down, and Jenny began to sing, in a strong, clear voice straight from the heart. Clara and Benjamin opened the kitchen door, giddy with pleasure. Tony watched, dumbstruck.

"More! More!" everyone called.

Tony held his hands up. "Let her eat, or she won't be strong enough to sing again." Tony took his place at the head of the table, with Jenny on his right, Baxter on his left.

The food began to arrive, and "Oohs" and "Ahs" came from the table. Tony called Benjamin and Clara into the dining room and toasted Clara as a wonderful cook, and Benjamin as the man who turned thorns into beauty. Clara pretended to taste her wine, excused herself and returned to the kitchen.

Benjamin pushed out the pie cart after the enormous dinner, and each guest had their favorite dessert. The young Back Road boys assisting Benjamin, filled the wine glasses.

After dinner, all guests went into the master parlor for wine and cheese, where Benjamin's helpers had rolled up the carpets, removed the furniture and lined the walls with chairs. Six huge crystal chandeliers lit the ceiling. The walls were papered with small red rosebuds; it had been Maria's favorite room in the house.

Musicians played a little jazz, some swing, and then a waltz, songs Jenny recognized from listening to Guy Lombardo and his Royal Canadians on her little radio.

Jenny danced her share as well, including an enchanting waltz with Tony.

Tony, who had started drinking before dinner, was now slurring his words. "Jenny," he warned her, "be careful with the wine. You're about the same size as my Maria, and she could only take three glasses."

As the dance ended, Tony fell over on Jenny's shoulder. Benjamin signaled the young men, who picked him up and carried him upstairs.

Exhausted but happy, the last guests finally said their goodbyes. Benjamin turned out the lights on the first floor.

Baxter walked upstairs with Jenny.

"Thanks, Jenny, for that beautiful song," Baxter said, leaning against the wall. He started to speak again, stopped and finally spoke up. "Jenny, what I did to you is my greatest regret. Please see me as I am now, and let's be friends." His voice cracked. "Please forgive me. I can make something of myself. I have goals and ambitions now."

Jenny felt a jolt through her body. *Do I dare believe that everything will be all right? Do I dare trust this man who tried to destroy me?*

Baxter steadied himself, wishing for a positive outcome. She looked up at him, not ready to give the answer he wanted, but knowing she had to say something.

"Baxter, I thank God that I survived you and other tormentors in my life. My future is in my own hands," Jenny said. She paused, then went on. "I accept your apology. You see, no matter what happens in my life, despite my getting knocked down, I always start again. You made your father proud tonight. I haven't seen Tony so happy in a long time. We've had a long evening. Goodnight, Baxter."

+++

The next two weeks were filled with Baxter and his friends in and out of the house. Baxter took Jenny went horseback riding three days before his furlough was over. She had never sat a horse. Baxter was an experienced horseman and tried to help her feel comfortable. They saddled a black and a chestnut, and rode off at a walk on a bridle path through woods.

She recognized his need to make up for the past.

"Baxter, today you've either added ten years to my life or taken ten off." She reached out a hand to him.

Tony stayed home, reading and walking the grounds. He and Baxter played cards until late at night. Clara spoiled everyone with all kinds of treats.

At breakfast on the day of Baxter's departure, Tony declared, "My God, Clara, I believe you're trying to kill us all." He had eaten four huge powdered biscuits, a slice of thick fried ham, two eggs sunny side up, and plenty of Clara's homemade strawberry jam.

"Clara," Baxter said mournfully, "how am I supposed to live on army rations after the past two weeks?"

"Well, I just might have to send you and your buddies a little care package."

Baxter went around the room, gave a hug to Clara and Benjamin and said goodbye. When he hugged Jenny, his last words to her were, "Thanks for forgiving me."

She looked straight into his blue eyes. "Baxter," she whispered, "you were a boy then; you are a man now. I prefer the man." He gave her a quick squeeze and hurried for the car.

+++

Jenny and Baxter wrote often. She pictured his camp, somewhere in the Ardennes Forest in Belgium. He told her the frigid weather was brutal, down to below freezing and eight inches of snow on the ground much of the time. The bombing runs were conducted in daylight, so the drops could accurately hit bridges and railway yards. His squad conducted their work under cover of darkness. Ice-covered faces, frostbite, trench foot, and exhaustion were common. Most of the tanks were camouflaged and hidden throughout the countryside. He even learned some of the local language from the farmers.

Baxter was sick, off and on, with stomach problems. He noticed his weight loss and experienced pounding headaches, but did not complain and continued as squad leader. He was good at his job and proud of his responsibilities. In one of his letters, he wrote, "I lived my childhood consumed with anger and fear and made a lot of mistakes. The army was a good idea."

On occasion, he mentioned the risk he took with each mapping mission. Late at night, he explored the countryside, bridges and road crossings, drawing maps for the destruction team's advancement to the next assault. The dangers were many, including enemy troops and land mines.

Weeks later, he wrote he was getting better at night-mapping and felt more confident in his job. More of the territory had been secured. With Baxter's mapping system, they had fewer casualties.

Late in September, a letter arrived from Baxter's commanding officer: Baxter was ill again and coming home on military leave if his condition didn't improve.

Tony arrived early one Friday afternoon after a long trip. Jenny overheard him talking to his attorney.

"I want to retire," he said. "I've sorted out the papers. My son and I want to test the real estate business. Baxter hates this racket."

"Are you sure? The business is making a large profit. Promote one of your captains. Take more time for yourself," replied the attorney.

Tony cleared his throat. "Things aren't the same since Sam's death. I'm the absent boss. That's no good for the family.

Now listen. Not a word of this conversation leaves this room. The last thing I need is a dead attorney." The attorney left with a pounding beat in his chest.

+++

One afternoon in early winter, Jenny was studying a business journal in the little study upstairs. She heard a car coming up the driveway and looked out the window, thinking Baxter was pulling an early surprise.

It was a military car with an insignia on the door. The same man she had seen two years ago got out.

Tony walked over to greet the visitor. They shook hands and looked at each other for a long moment.

Colonel Matthews said, "I'm sorry, Tony." He held a letter in his hand and gave it to Tony. "Let me just say that Baxter was a hero. He received the Silver Star."

Baxter did come home. *Never,* thought Jenny, *will any of us ever be the same.*

The funeral was overwhelming. Tony received the folded American flag with a face full of pure grief. Jenny struggled for something to say while fighting back tears. Nothing made sense anymore.

She had prayed Baxter would come home safe. She knew the snake incident forced Baxter's enlistment in the military; Tony gave him no choice. Everyone was happy that it had worked out for the best. How could Tony, how could *she*, ever forget that if it had not been for her, he would probably be alive today?

Tony locked himself in the library, on and off for days. He never ate at home, and everyone stayed out of his way. The mansion became a tomb.

Clara, Benjamin, and Jenny drove to the old cemetery every week. Sometimes, they talked and prayed. Other times, they cleaned the graves and planted flowers. Benjamin always left roses for Maria, Sam, and Baxter. All of their lives were cut short by tragedy. Tony never said good-bye to any of them. The three people visiting the graves knew Tony blamed himself for their deaths.

Doctor Stevens was the only non-business person to visit Tony. With the doctor, Tony shared the letter from the army about how Baxter died. An English-speaking German commando was placed in Baxter's company. He used captured US uniforms, trucks, and jeeps to camouflage his identity while becoming friends with several mapping squad members.

Baxter was slowly poisoned. They decided to speed things up when they found out he was being shipped home for rest. Before going out on a night mapping assignment, the spy had given Baxter an extra-strong dose. The poison caused Baxter to get separated from his squad. He ended up in an enemy camp. They tortured and mutilated him; he never gave military information. When he did not return to camp, a search party found his body deep in the forest.

+++

Over the next year, Tony spent many months in Hong Kong.

Jenny started a plan for her future. Most cities built cheap post-war prefab housing.

While listening to her favorite top ten billboard songs, she danced around the room to jazz and swing. Her favorite song was "It's Magic" by Doris Day.

She had saved enough money for several months' rent. Night work would be easy to get. Maybe in a government desk job researching files.

+++

When the war ended and wartime rationing was lifted in September 1945, prosperity did not immediately return. Many veterans needed work. Tony offered various jobs for bodyguards, drivers, bookkeepers, and merchant payment collectors. Most men preferred to stay with their old bosses.

People wanted new things. They wanted to put the war behind them. The government began to cut taxes, and added new construction budgets, causing an economic boom. Tuition was low, sometimes free at colleges and universities, for veterans under the GI Bill.

Most importantly, veterans returning with disfiguring injuries had new options for surgery to repair or replace their original scars.

CHAPTER FOURTEEN

The Unveiling

Jenny thought about resolving the unpleasant, painful past. Maybe people would look beyond her face if she became a secretary in charge of finding lost solders. Keeping busy while getting payed, could ease the memories of Baxter. She was thinking about Baxter and Jet when Dr. Stevens surprised her with a visit.

"Tony isn't here," she told him, without glancing up.

"I came to see you. Actually, Tony sent me."

"Well, I'm not sick, Dr. Stevens. Why would Tony send you?"

"Now listen, Jenny. This may be the only time you'll get this chance. Tony has arranged for the best plastic surgeon in the country to take a look at your face."

"What? Why?" Jenny raised her voice. "He hasn't said a word to me. Why would he, in God's name, want to do something for me? After all, I've been bad news for him since the first day he saw me."

"Listen, Jenny. Tony has plenty of money and power, and he's miserable. Maybe it will help him to help someone else. That's why he sent me. He can't talk to you about this.

"I'll arrange everything. I have a meeting for you and the plastic surgeon next Tuesday at 10:30 a.m. Do you understand what I'm saying? This is a chance for you to live a normal life. Let this doctor look at you. You have nothing to lose."

Over the next few days, Jenny was happy, sad, excited, then confused. With no one to tell about the situation, she appeared strange to Momma Clara and Benjamin. They noticed Jenny stopped studying her books.

Jenny packed her suitcase Monday evening, just in case, as Doctor Stevens suggested and left a note for Momma Clara. In the note, she stressed the need for secrecy. The car pulled up the driveway Tuesday, promptly at 10:00. Clara and Ben had gone to Back Road.

They went straight to the hospital and met Melody Princeton, who explained that her husband was Dr. Hugh Princeton and they worked as a team.

At once, Jenny relaxed. Dr. Princeton entered, and Melody lifted Jenny's veil. No one gasped.

Dr. Princeton asked, "Jenny, could you tell us how long your face has been damaged? It's an important part of the treatment process."

"About fifteen years, I think."

Dr. Princeton said, "It looks like a knife did most of the facial skin damage. The repair work left a lot of scarring." He thought for a moment. "Do you have family you want here with you?"

"No, Dr. Princeton, no one."

"Okay, Melody, let's take a look."

For over two hours, every inch of Jenny's body was examined, for areas to graft skin to rebuild her face.

Jenny did nothing except follow instructions. She tuned out the doctor and Melody. Instead, she pictured Momma Clara and Benjamin at the gravesites, church, and shopping together and realized how much she loved them. She knew they also loved her. "I wish Momma Clara, Ruth and Jet could be here."

"What?" Melody asked.

"Never mind," Jenny said. "Well, what's the verdict? Do I keep the veil?"

"I'll be honest with you, Jenny. Over the years, we've seen great improvements in facial restoration." Dr. Princeton hesitated. "This is going to take time and several surgeries. We'll need to use some cadaver skin. You'll have to remain at the hospital clinic for a very long time. Mr. Salvadore wants the best care for you. He made that perfectly clear. I want you to have a private-duty nurse after each operation. Without surgical complications, I think you'll be pleased."

The next week, following the admissions procedures, including a special diet, Jenny met her private nurse, Judy. She told Jenny she had taken care of several of Dr. Princeton's patients. They were happy with the results of their surgery.

Judy prepared Jenny for the operating room, and held her hand until the stretcher left her room.

Nearly eight hours later, Jenny came out of surgery.

On the third day, after some of the swelling had diminished, she lifted her hand and touched the bandage on her face. Her face felt tight, stinging and burning as if it were on fire.

She looked around the room and saw her nurse looking out the window. She tried to say, "Judy", but only a grunt came out. Then the nurse turned, and Jenny looked straight into the eyes of Ruth Stillman.

Ruth hurried over and took Jenny's hands. "Now, Jenny, don't move or you'll damage the repairs."

Jenny became hysterical, grabbing at Ruth until they gave her an injection to put her to sleep.

+++

Jenny woke, but kept her eyes closed. It was too good to be true that she'd thought Judy was Ruth. *Silly, really.* When she calmed down and opened her eyes, though, she still thought the drugs were playing tricks, because to her, Judy still looked like Ruth.

Ruth walked over to the bed. "Now, Jenny, you must be calm, or I'll have to get a shot for you again. Do you understand me?"

Moving her mouth was getting easier, and Jenny said, "Yes."

"Jenny, you're awake; you're not dreaming. I'm Ruth Stillman. I'm your friend." Ruth held both of Jenny's hands. "Jenny, I'll tell you everything, but you must be still. You won't help things by causing more trauma." Ruth waited until Jenny's fingers relaxed, and she knew Jenny would listen to her fairly and quietly.

"Okay. Your beautiful little boy Jet is now a handsome young man. He's at Boston University School of Law *on a full scholarship*. He lives on the campus." Even with full bandages on her face, Ruth could see in Jenny's brown eyes great happiness, as well as hurt, all the feelings of a mother.

After a few minutes, Ruth continued. "I've kept working, and Jet and I have been fine. He calls me Aunt Ruth. As he grew older, I couldn't keep pretending you were on a long trip. So, I told him there'd been a car accident, and you had died."

Ruth expected Jenny to show anger and shock at her, instead, tears wet the bandages around Jenny's eyes.

"Jenny," Ruth said, "your son is enrolled under his birth name, Jeremiah Elijah Thomas, and, yes, they still call him Jet. I made sure of that."

Jenny reached up and touched her friend's face. She mumbled indistinctly, "Picture?"

"Oh! Yes!" Ruth exclaimed. "Here in my wallet. Can you see well enough?" Carefully, Ruth supported Jenny with the soft pillows.

"Oh Ruth, oh, Ruth." Jenny held the picture to her heart. "I can't," Jenny said. "I can't believe I'm looking at my son." Her mood became electric. "I could only hope and pray all these years. I never lost hope."

Ruth leaned over and kissed Jenny on the forehead. Jenny reached up and put her arms around Ruth, and together, they cried.

+++

The restoration process, reshaping the bone structure of the jaw and chin and constant massaging to soften scar tissue left Jenny with bouts of extreme depression, but catching up on the past helped. Ruth and Jet led an ordinary life compared to Jenny's strange living arrangements. Ruth had kept a journal and pictures of Jet's life, and the information filled in a lost time for Jenny. Jenny told Ruth about finding Ruth's house, and almost getting arrested for being in the neighborhood.

"I think the veil caused suspicion; yet without it, my face caused fright."

One day as they sat by the window, Ruth asked, "Jenny, why is Mr. Salvadore doing this for you? Wouldn't he just want you to go away?"

Jenny grimaced and shook her head. "To be honest, I have the same thoughts. I never see anyone, so I don't have any answers. Dr. Stevens doesn't know. I know Tony considered me trouble, and sometimes a burden. I think he's doing it for Sam. If it works, maybe Tony and I can put the past behind us, and I'll get out of his way forever." She stared off into space.

Jenny enjoyed telling Ruth about Benjamin and Momma Clara. More than once Jenny asked to see them. She had a no-visitor order from Dr. Princeton, though he conceded that writing a letter wouldn't break the rules.

The following day, Jenny dictated, and Ruth wrote. At the end of the letter, Jenny requested that Momma Clara bring some jelly biscuits. "You haven't tasted Momma Clara's jelly biscuits, Ruth. If I could chew, you wouldn't get a single bite."

Jenny said, "Tell Momma Clara and Benjamin to keep the letter and visit a secret. They know how to keep secrets. They barely know the truth anymore."

"Well," Ruth answered, as she sealed the envelope, "as long as Mr. Salvadore is paying, we keep to the rules. Let's be careful during Dr. Princeton's visits. He can't know we were friends in the past. Remember, I only know you as your nurse. We can't afford the consequences if Mr. Salvadore found out the cause of your disfigurement."

The next day, after their usual walk in the clinic garden, Jenny said to Ruth, "Judy's coming back next week. What'll we do? I can't bear not to see you and talk about Jet."

"Well, my friend in crime," Ruth began in a sly tone. "First, I've been your nurse for over four months. I can still visit you. I often visit former patients. Second, I'll agree to work with you on Judy's days off. Your next phase of surgery is next week, and you'll need a private duty nurse around the clock.

"Now, according to Clara's letter yesterday, she and Benjamin will be here tomorrow. They'll visit while I'm still here, and it'll be the weekend, so the part-time staff will be too busy to notice, and they probably don't know all the housekeeping staff. I sent an orderly uniform for Benjamin and an aide's uniform for Clara."

"Oh, Ruth, I'm shaking all over," Jenny said. She ran over and looked into the mirror, surveyed her face with a pleased expression and gave a thumbs up to Ruth.

Ruth watched her best friend. *God, please take care of her. I love her so much.*

The next morning, Jenny could not rest. She was looking out the garden window when she heard a knock on the door.

Ruth opened the door. The black woman and man walked into the room. Jenny ran into the woman's arms and sobbed. "Momma Clara, I've missed you so much."

"My baby girl," Clara said. "Oh, Lord, Ben, look how thin my child is." Jenny let go of her finally and hugged Benjamin.

Jenny was like a different person during their visit. She talked non-stop. Clara fussed at Jenny, and they couldn't stop hugging each other. Everyone ate her biscuits; even Jenny managed a few crumbs. Happy, peaceful feelings filled the room.

"Everything is ready back at the house, and your Momma Clara needs to care for you," Clara said between hugs. She noticed the improvement to Jenny's face, where the bandages did not cover it. Some of the big railroad track scars were fading away.

Ruth promised to write them and reminded everyone to keep this day a secret. Momma Clara gave Jenny one long, last hug, with instructions to "do like that doctor tells you."

Jenny answered, "Yes, Momma."

+++

Weeks went by, with Ruth popping in and out.

Three months after Dr. Princeton used cadaver skin for the final surgery phase, Jenny was healing better than expected. A discharge date was set.

Jenny told Ruth about the discharge date when Judy went to the cafeteria for coffee.

"Give me the address," Ruth said. "I can visit you there. You mentioned his mansion is in the country, only about ten miles from the club. No one will be the wiser, and I'll do just about anything for more of those biscuits." They both laughed.

Two days later, Tony sent a car to bring Jenny and Judy to his house.

As they turned into the driveway, Judy looked amazed at the beautiful rose gardens bordering the entire drive.

"Oh, my," Judy exclaimed. "Your friend must be wealthy. This is unbelievable." The car stopped and Clara and Benjamin appeared. Immediately, Jenny was in Clara's strong arms.

Benjamin said, "Now Clara, you let Jenny get upstairs. She needs rest."

"Well, Jenny," Benjamin said, as he picked up her suitcase. "Welcome home."

They went upstairs, and Judy chose the bedroom next to Jenny's room for herself. She asked Benjamin if they'd see Mr. Salvatore, and he said they would. But his face was thoughtful as he went downstairs.

"Something sure smells good," he said, entering the kitchen.

"Uh-huh," Clara answered. "Did you put some roses in my baby's room?" she asked.

"First thing this morning. I probably should taste the ham and sweet potatoes," he said hopefully, then had second thoughts, noticing the butcher knife in Clara's hand.

"Have you ever seen nurse Judy before?" Ben asked.

"No," Clara said. "Why, Ben? Have you?"

Ben scratched his head, "I can't rightly put my finger on it. I sure thought she *looked* like somebody I seen before."

+++

Tony arrived just before dinner. Jenny had rested, bathed, and dressed in an outfit from her singing days at The Back Road Club.

She wore red silk trousers, a white silk long-sleeved blouse with red ruffles on the front, cuffs and collar. She also wore red high heels to look taller.

Her face was healing. A make-up artist at the recovery center had taught her to apply foundation and creams to conceal most of the heavy scarring. After so many years of avoiding the mirror, she enjoyed putting on the make-up, dressing and looking at herself. She'd stopped wearing the veil. Even though there was little sensation in her face, just touching her restored skin and looking into a mirror took her breath away.

Tony had not seen her in all this time. She was happy he chose not to visit. They didn't have much to say to each other.

Judy kept her uniform on and said she wasn't going to change for dinner. "I'm an employee, not a guest," she explained. "This is better."

Just before they were called downstairs, there was a knock on the door. "Come in," Jenny said.

"Well, well." Judy stood staring at Jenny. "You've outdone yourself! I wouldn't have recognized you! Let me brush those dark curls over your forehead. It'll cover the one noticeable scar line."

"Oh, Judy, do you really think this is okay?" Jenny asked as she turned around.

"Okay? Why, it's just plain gorgeous! This is a side of you I don't know."

Jenny laughed. "Well, let's take this side downstairs, I'm starving."

As they approached the dining room, Jenny saw Tony standing in front of Baxter's picture on top of the piano. The three happy people in the pictures, Maria, Sam, and Baxter, were all distant memories.

Hearing footsteps, Tony turned. Jenny and Judy walked toward him, smiling.

"Jenny," Tony spoke almost in a whisper. "Is it really you? My God, you are beautiful."

"Now, Tony," Jenny answered, "there's still more to do. Dr. Princeton hasn't released me yet, but very soon, I hope." She felt a little nudge on her shoulder.

"Oh, goodness, I almost forgot. Judy, this is Tony Salvadore. Tony, this is Judy, the best nurse ever."

"Hello," Judy said, smiling. "I'm glad to meet such a generous person. And Jenny is a delightful patient." Jenny saw Tony wink at Judy. *Was he really winking at her? Why? They just met.*

Early the next morning, Tony left for a family meeting at the club, and Jenny found Judy sitting in the brown leather recliner in the sunroom. She seemed oddly relaxed for a private-duty nurse. Jenny told herself she was being unduly suspicious.

+++

A month passed without complications. Dr. Princeton called and scheduled a visit. If Jenny continued improving, she would no longer require a private-duty nurse.

Three weeks later, the visit with Dr. Princeton was satisfactory. He was pleased with the results and satisfied with Jenny's ability to care for herself. Judy announced she would leave in the morning.

Jenny said good-bye to Judy at the front door and watched as Tony's chauffeur drove her and Tony away. *Was it a coincidence that Tony came downstairs, said goodbye, and left with Judy?*

Jenny ran to the phone. Ruth was coming tomorrow. They would have the entire day to talk about Jet. *Tonight, the stars will twinkle, and tomorrow, the sun will shine.*

Jenny looked out the front window every fifteen minutes. She recalled that Ruth's house was almost an hour's drive, the other side of the city. At last, a car pulled into the gravel driveway. As adrenalin rushed through her system, Jenny ran out the door and down the steps to Ruth.

Ruth and Jenny communicated largely by gestures, hugs and hands flying. They never tired of talking and laughing. Both helped Momma Clara wash clothes, make beds, clean, and dust.

Later that afternoon, Clara finished hanging out the wash and stretched her back. "Now, where did those young'uns go?" she muttered. "I just can't keep up with 'em." Then she heard voices in the kitchen and opened the door. The two sat at the table, an apple pie between them, with half missing and a fork in each hand.

"Now, look here," Clara scolded, "that pie was for supper. Look what you done." She picked up her wooden spoon. Jenny and Ruth jumped up, grabbed the pie and ran toward Ben, urging him to take it.

Clara didn't chase them, but her voice was loud enough for all three to hear her. "Tonight, you can just get in that kitchen and make do. I'll be in that big recliner with my feet up." Her laugh was crystal.

When Clara woke up an hour later, there was a beautiful bouquet of pink, red, white, and yellow roses, fresh from Ben's garden, next to her. She sat up, leaned over, touched and smelled the sweet fragrances.

"Well, I do declare, I just might fix a little meatloaf, in case company comes." Jenny, Ruth, and Ben came out from the other side of the sunroom with the empty pie plate.

"I'm sorry, Momma Clara," Jenny said, pretending guilt.

"Don't you start that with me." Clara took a deep breath. "Now that you're better, I'll make sure you earn your keep." Jenny kissed Momma Clara on the cheek and Ruth kissed the other cheek.

As they left, Ben came over and sat down. "Why Clara, I don't know when I've seen you so happy."

"Well, Ben, I do love that girl, like she was my own. I can't help it."

"I know," Ben answered. "I like her friend, Miss Ruth, too." Ben was quiet for a moment. "That Miss Judy gave me a strange feeling."

"You too?" Clara said. "I thought it was just me. Still, she took good care of my baby. She must be a good nurse."

+++

Ruth told Jenny about Jet. He would finish law school in two years. "Jenny," Ruth asked one evening as they were saying good-bye, "will you ever meet Jet?"

"Absolutely not. I have gone too far to start causing him trouble now," Jenny said. "I've not been afraid for myself. I am afraid for you and Jet."

"But, Jenny, how can you want to see him so much and not go?"

"Because the mob murdered my husband and nearly killed me. I know they think I'm dead. I can deal with this a helluva lot easier knowing my son is safe. Should Tony find out about Johnny working for Marty and all the information about the prostitution connection, Jet and I would become targets."

"I understand," Ruth said and gave Jenny a hug. "Keep putting those compresses on at least three times a day. We want you to keep healing," Ruth instructed as she drove away. The seconds ticked past, then a final good-bye wave.

"My son." Those were words Jenny couldn't say to anyone, except Ruth. "*I have a son. I am the mother of a wonderful, handsome young man.*" She went upstairs to write another letter to Jet. It was one of hundreds she'd written, but never mailed. She gave them to Ruth to store. Someday, she might want them.

CHAPTER FIFTEEN

The Moving

"Well, then, it's time," Tony said beaming. For the fifth consecutive day, he was urging Jenny to go with him to the club. "You *need* to get out of this house. I insist."

Jenny shrugged. She didn't trust Tony, and she walked on eggs around him.

It wasn't her looks that worried her now. Dr. Princeton had performed miracles with her face, even if the rest of her body was still scarred, especially after all the skin grafts. No, she did not think about her looks now.

During her recovery, she thought about her future. She wasn't so naïve as to believe Tony did this out of kindness or compassion. She understood there would be payback. *If I had to do it over, I would still do it.*

Tony told her the outcome was amazing. "Your new face must be 'similar' to the other face of Jenny." She was a little peeved with the look from Tony, treating her like one of his conquests.

Well, I am bored staying in the house all the time. And Ruth has been too busy to visit lately.

"I think I'll go out." Her eyes were wide and questioning accepting his invitation.

She chose an outfit to give her strength:

A crimson fitted dress with Gibson girl sleeves, back out, with netting and wide black collar shaping into a V-neck in front. Jenny wore a size six. The long lace-up red flat ghillies tied in front and were great for dancing. She made up her face, and finally put on a thin, net veil. *I'm going to wear it, take it off, and silence all the whispers Sam hid from me.* When she looked into the full-length mirror for a last look, she was so delighted, she almost cried.

There was a knock on the door. "It's just me honey," said the voice that always felt like a hug to Jenny.

"Come in, Momma Clara. I'm ready."

Clara walked in. "Oh! My beautiful baby!" Jenny took a turn around for her.

"Now, listen, honey. You always been pretty to me. Now everybody can see what I been seeing, but no need for my baby to wear that veil anymore."

"I know," Jenny said. "It'll be a surprise." She removed the veil and held it in her hand.

"Jenny," came a loud voice from the end of the stairs.

"She's coming, Mr. Tony," Clara answered. "Well, honey, you have yourself a good time, but be careful." She gave Jenny a hug.

Tony stared admiringly at Jenny and took her hand. They walked arm in arm to the car. Tony had champagne waiting inside and poured them each a glass. They drank to new beginnings, and Jenny put on the veil and explained the surprise she wanted to share at the club.

Jenny had never seen Tony so relaxed. Everyone had been told she was recuperating from an illness at Tony's house. Whatever else they knew, that was the story they told Jenny.

Tony was a great dancer, and dance they did. After so many bitter years, Jenny felt finally free of pain and shame.

She was feeling appreciative and a little drunk. She decided to go up to the band and offered to sing for Tony.

When the band leader announced Jenny, the Siren, she saw Tony's jaw tighten. He remained in his seat, as though he approved of her behavior.

Jenny sang *Sentimental Journey,* and all conversation ceased. The band was right with her, and the moment was magical.

She finished, took a bow, and heard the applause. When Tony stood up, Jenny spoke into the microphone. "This little siren needs a rest." Everyone laughed. She waited a moment and then lifted the veil.

She didn't worry about what they'd expected to see, though there was a sudden hush from the crowd. She just said, "Thank you," and let them stare as she and Tony took their seats.

Tony was quiet on the way home. She hummed softly. The evening had been perfect. She was tired and a little intoxicated. Most of all, she felt, *I'm back, and life can be marvelous again.*

+++

The next day, Tony left for three weeks in Hong Kong. The plastic surgery made her believe in herself again, but she was no nearer financial independence. She could take a job during the daytime now but refused any opportunity to work in the medical field.

"After my ordeal in hospitals, I don't want to work in one, maybe a physician's office later." Jenny didn't have the right answer yet but trusted it would turn up.

Late on a hot, steaming night, as Jenny sat at her opened window, listening to her favorite band music echoing from The Back Road Club, she discovered the answer.

She approached Tony on his return with her plan. She would entertain at his club as a paid employee.

To her surprise, Tony didn't turn her down right away. "Well," he said, "I *could* use the talent. You don't have experience as a performer, but everyone liked your style. I agree to this arrangement for the present."

Jenny was thankful she had kept The Back Road Club a secret, except from Baxter. Now, it would come in handy.

She felt a great sense of release. *I'll work at the club for a short time, renew my classes and never look back!*

+++

Over the weeks, Tony allowed Jenny to maintain her own schedule and trusted her attention to the patrons. She requested no special favors, and her assistance made his life easier.

Jenny mailed money to Ruth on every payday and requested it be used for Jet. She passed her driver's examination and between her savings and her new income, she put a down payment on a 1952 red hard-top Ford Victoria, which cost $1,650. She chose to pay for it in installments. At last, she began to feel freedom from her cluttered past. She didn't need any financial assistance from anyone for this purchase.

After months of her daily routine, Tony asked her to go to several businesses to pick up packages for him.

"I'll increase your wages to $2496 annually. It'll help pay for gas," he said slowly.

"Okay. Just give me the addresses and shopping list," she said. She was bored with hanging around the club all day. The extra errands would be welcome.

Jenny began to feel real relief from the pain and anguish of her dependence, and the beginning glimmers of freedom. She was incredibly proud of her progress.

She and Tony were not lovers, nor ever considered it. There had been only one true, committed love for each of them; Maria for Tony, Johnny for Jenny.

Tony was about twenty years older than Jenny, but in no way a father-figure. They were friends without any further commitment. With each day, Tony knew that Jenny was counting the weeks till she could leave his house for good.

+++

Later that year, Tony started completing large international deals at his home. Sometimes, he gently insisted Jenny attend the meetings, where she composed notes and recorded the names of attendees for his records. After a few drinks, she excused herself.

Jenny had no time, no interest, in the club's business affairs. She enjoyed performing and loved her job counting money in Tony's office. She was impressed with his wealth and influence. She pushed control of melancholy feelings. Her diary entry communicated her determination very clearly. Someday, she hoped it would explain missing pieces of her life to her son.

+++

One rare day, when Tony was at home, he announced he had a surprise for her birthday. Jenny created her birth date a long time ago.

"Come on," he said, "let's go for a little drive."

The car stopped in front of a three-story brick apartment building with a beautiful small yard, shrubbery and flowers out front. Jenny knew the area. It was within walking distance of the club.

The driver opened the door. Tony helped Jenny out and put a set of keys in her hand.

"It's yours," he said. "I floated you a loan. Show me around."

"What?" Jenny exclaimed! "What's mine?"

"The whole building. You're your own landlord," Tony said. "Now, let's go inside."

Jenny opened the door and entered the lobby. The man at the reception desk had been informed by Tony that Jenny was the new landlord. He pushed another set of keys into her hand.

"Good to see you, Miss Stone. Welcome. One set is for the front door and the other is to your suite."

"My suite?"

"Yes, ma'am, suite 100 on the main floor. When you have time, I'll tell you about your two tenants. I'm your building manager." He began to talk quickly and fluently. "My name is Grady Rogers; everyone just calls me Roger. Mr. Tony, I let those furniture people in, like you told me, and no one else."

"Thanks," Tony said. "Now, Jenny, let's go see where you'll be living."

Tony escorted her down a carpeted hall, with flowers in vases on end tables and bright pictures on the walls. They stopped in front of the door with the number 100 in a brass plate.

"Go ahead, Jenny, see if the key fits." It did. She strolled into her own new apartment.

Jenny excitedly opened the door to each room. She observed everything, walking and taking mental notes. A peek outside included a cute, plant-bordered patio. *This will require a little help from Benjamin.* The other two apartments, on the second and third floor, had balconies. Jenny stood in the modern kitchen.

"Jenny, I've owned this for some time. It's just a damn headache to me now. I'm selling it to you."

"Tony, there's no way I have that kind of money, not to mention the furniture costs."

"Well, Jenny, you're a highly motivated woman, and judging from many hints, you're ready to move out of my house. There will be income from the other tenants, about $2160 yearly.

You'll make monthly payments on the building. This is not a gift; it's a business opportunity. I signed the building over to you. I don't have the desire or time to be a landlord. God knows, I have enough on my plate with the Hong Kong industry."

"Well," Jenny said. "Maybe I can take this hardship off your hands. But I insist on a business plan; I don't want handouts, Tony."

They agreed his lawyer would send her the contract. Then Jenny had something else to say. "Now, Tony, listen. I cared for Sam, and he loved me; not *in* love, but caring for each other. I know he cared. Sam didn't turn away from me when I needed help the most. And you know what else?"

"What?" He appeared genuinely interested.

"Sam and I could have made it. For better or worse, we could have worked it out. We had just begun to get to know each other, I mean, really getting to know each other, before he died." Jenny sat on the sofa.

Tony looked around the room. "There's no family left for me, Jenny. Business is all that matters to me. Let's stop looking back and start moving forward. Why don't you get settled? I'm going back to the club."

As he closed the door quietly, she knew he could now arrange her life if he chose. She had no idea what he was setting in motion for her.

Thank goodness Tony had a phone installed. She immediately called Ruth.

"What did you just say?" Ruth thought she had misunderstood. "An apartment building? Where, how, why?" A feeling of utter horror surged through Ruth.

"Ruth, slow down. I want you to come over as soon as you can." She gave her phone number, address, and directions to Ruth.

"Does this mean you don't live at Tony's anymore?" Ruth asked.

"You bet," Jenny answered. "I have been planning a move. After all, living in Tony's house requires me to obey his requests rather than pursuing my own interest. Of course, I need to make payments. I think I make enough at the club for that. Come on over and we'll go to Tony's for my things. I need to tell Momma Clara."

"Well," Ruth said. "That should go over well. Miss Clara is going to be mighty upset."

"Oh, she'll get over it," Jenny responded. "She'll be so proud that I have my own place."

+++

Clara and Benjamin huddled on the sofa. Jenny carefully explained, there would be a change in her life, her business with Tony, including the apartment building. She felt a slow throb of pain go through her body. Ruth sat in the corner of the large living room, looking at the cloudy day. The dark and gloom outside leaked into the faces inside the house. The wind blew softly-moving branches against the house.

"I don't see why you're not happy for me, Momma Clara. I can't live here without working and helping out. This isn't my home. Tony could make me leave anytime. It's like living on the edge, according to Tony's moods." She hugged Momma Clara. "I need you to be proud and happy that I'm on my own. Please say you'll come visit me. I have lots of room for guests."

Clara turned and looked earnestly at Jenny.

"Well," she said, "I suppose I've seen it coming." You want a home of your own. It's natural enough." *I will not bust this beautiful girl's hopes.*

"Sure, honey," Momma Clara said. "Go get your things and I'll fix you a little something to eat in your new home."

"Come on, Ruth," Jenny said. "If you expect to eat, you need to work." The two raced up the stairs, laughing and talking; the sounds made Clara momentarily happy.

Clara and Ben went to the kitchen. Ben had been under the weather. Jenny hadn't noticed Ben not saying much. The doctor said it was age. Clara knew Ben was becoming more and more forgetful, and he never seemed hungry anymore. With Miss Maria, Mr. Tony, Mr. Sam, Mr. Baxter and now Jenny gone, there wasn't much need for Ben to keep the rooms full of his beautiful roses. He enjoyed going to church, but lately he started finding excuses to stay in bed and miss Sunday services.

Well, time does have a way of changing things. She wiped her hands on her apron, looked at Ben sleeping in the chair, and began to fix some chicken and dumplings. They were Jenny's favorite.

+++

Where had the time gone? It had been almost two years since Jenny moved into the apartment building. She proved a quick learner and a disciplined businesswoman. With Roger's help, collecting the rent from the other tenants, singing at the club and running errands for Tony, the old feelings of isolation and loneliness occurred less and less. I know Tony is trying to control me. I can't leave yet, until I have everything the attorney general's office will need for a conviction, facts without any doubt. Also, this information cannot come from me. My name in the papers will bring attention to Johnny's killers. Her annual income totaled about $4600.

Most of Jenny's income went to help pay Jet's expenses. She needed to be part of Jet's life. Now he had an old Buick to drive and gave all his thanks and hugs to Aunt Ruth. She said she had sold some property and received the first payment.

Jet never questioned her. He was graduating in two weeks and would start working as an assistant prosecutor for the district attorney's office. As class valedictorian, he could pretty much get the job of his choice. He preferred to prosecute criminals rather than defend them.

To Jet, the law was simple. Everyone knew the boundaries. Step over the limits; welcome to the consequences. He was building a political future. His internship for the state of New York during law school provided a clean, clear key to the good life.

+++

Ruth was entering the house as Jet was leaving.

"I left something on the table you might want to see," he said, with a joking grin. She saw the same smile in Jenny. They really were two of a kind.

She put another letter from Jenny to Jet in the storage boxes in the basement. Ruth carefully dated each box. She knew one day Jet would read them and understand the amazing woman who wrote them.

She opened the manila envelope on the table. It was Jet's graduation photograph.

What a handsome young man! Dark curly hair, blue eyes, olive complexion, and that smile of confidence and happiness. She grabbed the envelope and took it to show to Jenny.

Ruth knocked on Jenny's door. Two voices inside were arguing loudly: Tony and Jenny.

"I won't, and you shouldn't ask me!" Jenny shouted.

"Jenny, calm down. I'm in a bind, for God's sake. This could be both a business opportunity and a great travel experience. Try it once. If you hate it, don't go again.

"My 'foundation' helps these girls. Hong Kong is crowded, and these girls are refugees and cheap labor. I need them welcomed by a woman. I prefer a nurse, but Judy couldn't exactly time her mother's death, could she? All I ask is a little compassion, as they get off the Goddamn plane.

I can't trust anyone else. These girls will go to Chicago in two weeks. Is that too much to ask of a friend?"

"Damn you Tony, I told you!" Jenny threw her hands over her head. "This is the part of the business you and Sam did. I *do not, and will not, be involved.* Didn't I make myself clear three months ago, when I helped out then? I told you I wouldn't do it again."

"Helped out?" Tony said. "All you did was take names and give out new ones at a desk. Big deal. You never even went to see the girls, and I paid you well for that. But no, you don't want to help out a friend, let alone a girl who could be your daughter's age, if you had one."

"Get out! Get out, Tony! I'm content with my life."

"I'm leaving. But think about it. I still have three weeks until they get here."

Ruth quickly hid behind the building as Tony came out and waited until his car was out of sight, then knocked on the door.

"Jenny, it's Ruth. Open the door."

The door opened. Jenny had a cigarette and a mixed drink in her hand.

"Come in. Can I fix you something?"

"No," Ruth replied. "Looks like you're having a rough day."

"You might call it that," Jenny said. "I'm spending a fortune on damn Marlboro cigarettes at twenty-five cents a pack. But it helps. Hey, what's that in your hand?"

Jenny took the envelope, opened it, and dropped the drink and the cigarette.

"What's the matter?" Ruth asked.

"Oh Ruth, this is my Johnny." Jenny held the picture to her chest.

"Jenny," Ruth said. "That's Jet. He is graduating in two weeks, and that's his graduation photo. You mean that's how Johnny looked?"

"Down to the last detail."

Ruth used a dustpan to remove the cigarette and glass from the floor. "I think we need a drink." She began filling the glasses.

"Graduates in two weeks?" Jenny repeated.

"Yes," Ruth said. "It's going to be on the front lawn of the law school. You could come and see the ceremony."

"How?" Jenny asked. "I don't want anyone to see me."

"Let's drive over in a few days and find a spot for the best mother of the best graduate to watch, and not be watched. It'll take about six hours and we can get in a lot of gossiping during the trip."

Two days later, on a warm day in May with the sun shining, and every tree around Boston University School of Law in bloom, Ruth and Jenny circled the campus.

"Drive over there," Ruth pointed. "That's where the ceremony will be held." They parked the car and walked to the lush lawn.

"Now," Ruth said. "Jet explained that all the parents and friends will be seated in chairs on the lawn. Each student has two tickets. Jet invited his girlfriend Amy to the ceremony, along with me."

"His girlfriend!" Jenny exclaimed. "This is the first time you've mentioned a girlfriend!" *My little boy has a girlfriend.*

"They met at a law seminar. She's graduating from Tennessee with a law degree. She worked her way through law school. I believe she plans to work on the opposite side of the court room."

"What do you mean, 'the opposite side'?" Jenny asked.

"Well, Amy plans to defend, and—these are Jet's words—the criminals–you know–she'll be a defense attorney."

"Good grief," Jenny said. "That should make for interesting dinner talk. What do you know about her, Ruth? What about her parents?"

"Hold on, Mother dear. They've only been dating for a short time. It's a long-distance relationship. I'll meet her parents at graduation. And now that you know, go ahead and prepare questions for me," Ruth smiled. "Let's find the right spot for you to watch."

Jenny looked around. "Ruth, look at that tree. Jet's last name begins with T, so he'll walk over this way and then down the aisle. I can park my car over there and leave before the crowd starts disbanding... Ruth, are you listening?"

"Yes, Jenny, but it's just not right. You should be sitting down there, not hiding behind a damn tree."

"Now, listen, Ruth Stillman. We have not gone to hell and back to give it all up for selfish reasons."

"But Jenny, why do we still have to be so careful?"

"Ruth, until Tony is behind bars or dead, the fact that I'm Jet's mother, or that I even *know* him, could cost him his life. They'll use me to get at him. I've held him in my arms a million times in my dreams, said his name and felt his little arms around my neck. I ache for just the *sight* of him, and I love him as much as any mother sitting in those seats. Jet has his mother's best friend to sit in that seat,

159

who watched over my son and continued his life. I love you, Ruth Stillman."

+++

Oh, Jenny, if I could only tell you. There will only be one love for me, my darling. And raising your son is the dream of a lifetime.

CHAPTER SIXTEEN

The Graduate

Saturday, May 7, 1955 presented a beautiful, soft breeze spring day in Boston. Jenny remained grateful and joyful, but her mind felt a sense of urgency.

She felt her main mission was to secure her son's safety. *Please God, don't let me do anything foolish,* she prayed silently.

Jenny dressed in a conservative red and white polka-dot dress with bracelet length sleeves and stockings with sandals.

Ruth had given her the graduation program, and through happy tears, she read the name she gave her baby on the list of graduates: **Jeremiah Elijah Thomas**. Jet was also the class valedictorian. *Yes, Johnny, our son will be a practicing attorney.*

"We're going to cry like two old women," Ruth warned her. Jenny knew she was right.

She sat quietly in her car, as people filled the chairs on the lawn. She looked over and spotted Ruth. They had agreed not to recognize or signal each other in any way.

+++

Two days ago, she had given Ruth a gift for Jet, along with another letter for the basement box. It was an expensive gold Elgin square-faced wristwatch. She'd wanted to give it to him and see his face when he opened it. She could only imagine the moment.

Ruth left the box in his room at home and agreed to pretend it came from her, as Jenny instructed.

Jet had mentioned he and Amy might share an apartment after graduation. Ruth chose not to mention this information to Jenny. *All in good time,* she decided.

The band started to play. Jenny got out of the car and walked to her tree.

Jenny saw Ruth sitting down front. For a moment, she envied her best friend, and just as quickly, she felt all the love this precious friend had given her son. Ruth had gone far beyond friendship.

Jenny almost collapsed when she saw him. Jet was smiling and looking around for Ruth and Amy. When he glanced toward her, Jenny took a step backward and nearly lost her footing.

She listened to her son's speech. He thanked his Aunt Ruth; there was no mom and dad. Jenny soaked up Jet's words like a sponge.

The University president began to announce the graduates. Jenny's chest hurt with pride. She stumbled back to the car.

The graduation ceremony ended. Jenny looked over and saw Ruth and Jet hug each other. Amy and apparently, her parents, greeted Ruth and Jet.

Jenny started the motor, turned on the air conditioning, and cried all the lonely trip home.

I feel abandoned. There is nothing I can do but work harder at getting away from Tony, and remain alive. There is an escape route. I will see my son; I will talk to my son. This will be done while I am alive. Yes, I'm afraid. Give me strength, Lord, she prayed.

She went into her apartment, lit a cigarette and fixed a scotch and soda. She wanted desperately to be included.

Jet was starting a new life. She had been such a tiny part of his other life. Oh, Johnny, why didn't you know, *or did you know?* I have a heart and it hurts so much.

She shouted to the walls, "This should have been *my* special moment! It's not right!" The more she thought, the more she drank. A dark shadow entered her body, mind, and spirit.

CHAPTER SEVENTEEN

The Trouble

During the month following Jet's graduation, Jenny could not escape her deep depression.

Jenny surrendered to it; she drank day and night, sadness soaking her body. Then one day, lying in a stupor, she dimly heard keys opening her door and people talking inside. She felt herself being carried outside. Then, mercifully, she blacked out.

She spent a week in an alcoholic detox at a treatment center. She began to physically feel stronger, but dark despair remained a formidable enemy. She missed several individual counselling sessions and refused group therapy. She left the center against medical advice.

+++

The summer passed. Ruth seldom visited. Jenny spent more time at the club, taking over most of Tony's record-keeping. If she drank too much, she slept on the sofa in Tony's office.

+++

In September of the following year, Jenny read the newspaper headline that her son would replace the retiring lead prosecutor in the District Attorney's office. There was a handsome picture of Jet, with some tough talk about cracking down on mob crime. The article ended with a list of guilty verdicts considered prosecution victories.

She wished she could feel joy for him, but the darkness was pushing down on her again.

+++

A few days later, Tony casually asked her to accompany him to Hong Kong.

"Sure, why not?" she replied. "I've never been on a plane, and I need to start living, right?"

The trip was wonderful. They stayed at the Peninsula Hotel in Hong Kong. While Tony took care of business, Jenny shopped and played tourist.

She told Tony the next evening over dinner, "Just leave me here. I love getting away from everyone."

"Well, you can stay for another week, if you want, and also do me a small favor," Tony replied.

"I'll do anything. I don't want to go home yet," Jenny pleaded.

"Well," Tony began, "I have several girls ready to travel to the States. They have their tickets, and I'll have someone help you with the language."

Jenny looked at Tony. "Tell me again. Why are we helping girls in Hong Kong and using your money to do it? How will you ever get your money back?"

"Jenny, I just help them get started in the States. I can't control their every move. Sometimes the girls get entertainment contracts and they pay a little to the club," Tony answered.

Jenny wasn't interested in their work habits. "All right, I'll go take a look for you." She needed this time away from Tony to overcome the increasing feeling she was paddling backward.

As soon as she thought that, she drank the thoughts away. Tony helped her to her room and put her to bed.

Tony flew back to New York the following day, leaving Jenny several pages of typed instructions and a generous amount of money.

Jenny left her hotel that morning with a pounding hangover and sat on the hotel bench nearby, trying to recover. She heard beautiful music and saw a boy about fifteen years old, wearing a dingy white t-shirt, sandals, and dark loose-fitting pants on his slender frame. He was making the music with an instrument resembling a bamboo stick and when the piece was done, he approached her with a quick bow and handed her a piece of paper. It was from Tony; *he* was the person paid to help her with the language.

Tony had provided a car and driver. They drove outside the city limits. The car stopped, the boy opened an iron gate, and they drove up to a mansion.

The boy took her into a dimly-lit room, where she saw girls everywhere: putting on make-up, painting their faces, dressing, sewing and laughing. Others were wrapping their feet; they were the smallest feet she had ever seen.

The boy quietly walked between two curtains that divided the room and motioned her to follow. In the second room, she smelled burning incense.

A voice spoke out of a cloud of smoke. "Miss Jenny Stone, come in, come in."

Jenny walked toward the voice. A wrinkled Chinese woman stood smoking a cigarette in a long, elegant holder.

"Please, sit down." The woman motioned to a stack of beautiful patterned cushions on the floor, and Jenny sat. The young boy removed her shoes and left. The small round table held a teapot and cups. The woman clapped her hands, and a girl appeared, bowed, poured tea, bowed again and left.

The small woman spoke perfect English. "You have the papers, Jenny Stone?"

"Yes, yes, I do." Jenny gave her the envelope.

"Well," the woman continued as she read, "I believe everything is in order." She took a pen from the sleeve of her embroidered Cheung Sam and signed the papers.

"Now," she said, "you must sign also."

Jenny looked at the papers, wishing she had read them. Tony never mentioned she had to sign anything. *Well, too late. I need to get out of here.*

She signed Jenny Stone under the woman's name: Anna Le. They each signed a second copy. The woman toasted her, wishing her a safe journey. Jenny pretended to drink her tea. The woman clapped her hands, and the same girl reappeared and bowed. She returned Jenny's shoes and motioned her to leave.

The young boy was waiting at the car.

As they drove through the city, Jenny read the rest of Tony's instructions, which was mostly just the travel schedule, with a short note in his handwriting.

Don't lose any girls. Tony.

Well, that won't be difficult. I don't have *any girls. I left them with the creepy lady.*

The following week, Jenny enjoyed sightseeing and shopping before her journey ended. She knew she had found her safe house, if needed. One afternoon, she looked up to the foreign sky into a mass of dark clouds.

"Look, Jenny," she said aloud, "you need to wake up! Tony lives in a world of tragedy and sin.

He gave you a pathway! Now, you are familiar with air travel. Gather your conviction evidence, mail the information to Jet. With Tony in prison, if you succeed, you'll be a free woman! Now, show courage, complete the business course that has been on hold, and *separate* from Tony, once and for all!"

Arriving at the airport to fly home, she was surprised to see the boy waiting for her, with at least ten girls, all talking at once, also at the terminal.

Jenny looked at them closely. They had to be teenagers. My God, one looks like she's not even ten years old. Are they orphans?

Jenny smiled at the girls. They appeared fearful, unsure what to do.

Jenny asked the boy, "Are these girls going with me to America?" He nodded yes.

He spoke to the girls and took several pictures of them, using Jenny's new Polaroid camera. Jenny gave the picture showing all of them to the youngest girl.

She kept them close to her, took them to their assigned seats, and made sure they had something to eat. She tried to say goodnight, and the youngest girl started to cry. Jenny held her in her arms until she quieted down.

I understand now. Tony set me up for this. I'll never do this again. Of course, I've never seen any Chinese girls at the club, but I'm suspicious of his relocation program. I intend to try and locate the whereabouts of the small girl in about a month.

After two transfers, they boarded the last flight for home.

They were met at the airport by a woman Jenny had never seen, who gave Jenny a letter identifying her as Martha Hawthorne, with The Refugee Relocation Foundation. Slowly, she collected the girls and put them on a waiting bus.

Jenny took one last picture as the girls entered the vehicle.

Back at her apartment, as Jenny prepared for bed, she saw a mountain of boxes stacked in her guest bedroom.

"What the hell?" Then she saw a note on the bedside table.

Just need to store these damn records some place. Someone is coming for them in a few days. Yes, I expect there'll be a storage fee. Tony.

Jenny shuddered. Tony either had a key to her apartment, or Roger had let him in. *Well, we'll set that straight tomorrow, Mr. Roger.*

Jenny took the sleeping pills the club doctor had given her. Everyone working for Tony also saw Dr. Jamison.

The following night, she performed at the club, wearing her signature red outfit for strength. Tony always introduced Jenny as the "Red Siren". She enjoyed dreaming up ways to wear red. Having her own dressmaker helped a lot.

She completed her degree while working in the club at night. She was building up quite a savings account, which she kept secure in her deposit box.

Late one night, she felt too exhausted to walk home. She had enjoyed the walk to the club in the early evening, now she realized that was not the brightest idea. Charlie and Speedy, her favorite club bouncers, offered her a ride.

"We're going your way after one stop, Jenny," Charlie said.

They drove across town, with Jenny mumbling in the back seat, then she drifted into sleep. She had stopped drinking alcohol after Hong Kong, deciding this was her one way out, to take back control of her life.

Two hours later, Jenny woke up. "Where am I?" She sat up and saw Charlie walking out of a warehouse.

"Hey, Jenny. Can you drive?"

"Drive? Where are we going?"

"To your house, as soon as Speedy gets here."

Jenny got out of the car. The cool air made her feel better; her headache was gone.

Speedy came out and leaned against the car. *Is that blood on his coat?*

"Speedy," Jenny asked, "are you hurt?" He held up a gloved hand and Jenny saw he was holding a gun.

He said, "Here, take this." Jenny took the gun, and threw it in the back seat.

Charlie and Speedy laughed. "For God's sake, Jenny! It isn't loaded," he said. "Not anymore."

"What happened, Speedy?" she asked.

"Well, we were moving boxes and something in one of them cut my hand. It's really nothing, I just bleed a lot."

"I want to go home *now!*" Jenny demanded.

"Okay, okay. You drive, Jenny."

Jenny got behind the wheel and sped off, with Charlie and Speedy in the back. In less than two blocks a police car pulled behind them, with blue lights on.

"For Christ's sake!" Speedy said. "I don't know the cops here. Shit, Jenny, you shouldn't be speeding. You have to lose 'em." Charlie and Speedy crouched in the back seat.

"Are you crazy?" Jenny said, gripping the wheel.

She tried to slow down, and Charlie screamed at her. "Get going, you fool! If they catch us, we're all go to prison for life!"

"Oh, my God!" Jenny pushed the gas pedal down, as hard as she could. She had no idea which way to go. With tires screeching, she turned into the path of an early delivery truck.

The driver slammed on the brakes and clipped the back of the car. Her face hit the steering wheel, and she tasted blood from her cut lower lip.

Speedy and Charlie were tossed from one side of the car to the other. She passed an alley, backed up and sped down and out the other end. A quick left and they went across the bridge toward the club.

It was close to five a.m. when Jenny pulled into the club parking lot, the sound of her heartbeat thrashing in her ears.

"I'll be damned," Speedy said. "She lost the sons of bitches. Now, I call that *some* driving."

Jenny got out of the car, ran the two blocks to her apartment, and went inside.

+++

Just before 10:00 a.m. on Wednesday morning, the terror played its cards.

Jenny turned her 1950 RCA radio on and sat on her sofa reading the paper. She saw a brief article about a double murder on Cedar Street two days before.

As she read on, she knew without a doubt that she had been there in the car, waiting for Charlie and Speedy. The article stated the stolen getaway car was found abandoned in an alley. She became aware that the radio carried the same news.

She jumped up, paced back and forth. "I'll call Ruth, she'll know what to do." She had hardly spoken to Ruth in the last year, but as always, she turned to her without question.

+++

Ruth almost hung up without even speaking. The person on the phone was sobbing, talking without making any sense.

"Who is this?" Ruth demanded.

"It's Jenny, Ruth, it's Jenny!"

171

"What is it, Jenny?" Ruth asked.

Jenny managed to say, "Help me, Ruth, please help me," and hung up.

Ruth threw her coat on and rushed out the door.

+++

A voice bellowed over a bullhorn. "Open up! FBI! Open up, Jenny Stone! We know you're in there!"

"Not until Ruth gets here." She tried to control the terror taking over her body.

She heard a key unlock the door and watched Roger let people into her apartment.

They grabbed her coat. She reached for her purse.

"Leave it," the FBI agent said, holding onto Jenny's arm. Flashbulbs blinded her when they left the apartment.

+++

Ruth turned onto the street to Jenny's apartment and saw blue lights flashing everywhere. The police had the street barricaded. She watched men wearing jackets with an FBI insignia on the back enter Jenny's building.

She pulled her car to the curb; thankful she wore her nurse's uniform and name tag. A policeman walked over to her. Ruth rolled her window down.

"I'm sorry, Miss, you can't go down this street."

"What's wrong, Officer? I'm a trained nurse. I have a patient on this street."

"Well, you'll need to call them. I can't let anyone in or out. Who's your patient?" the officer asked.

Ruth said at once, inventing a name out of thin air, "Mr. Mark George, but I guess I could visit tomorrow. Is someone hurt?" Ruth asked.

"No, ma'am," he replied. "The FBI is in charge. This street closing is their order."

Ruth was about to drive away when she saw flashbulbs going off and FBI agents escorting Jenny out. Jenny held her head down and wore her long red velvet coat. Several men carrying boxes followed close behind.

As the policeman motioned, Ruth turned the car around and went home.

CHAPTER EIGHTEEN

The Hard Case

In the past two years, Jenny's activities at the club had put a severe strain on her relationship with Ruth.

On a rare visit, Ruth questioned Jenny, "Aren't you afraid of Tony's activities? What he's doing *must* be illegal."

Jenny shrugged. "I almost have enough money for a down payment on a little house. With a new job, and this building, which I own, any bank will float me a mortgage for the rest. I'm not worrying about Tony anymore. I have plans for him and his evil connections."

Ruth spent the night in prayer: the love of her life was hurt and in trouble.

She had told Jenny about Jet's engagement to Amy. Jenny had read the announcement in the paper. Jet was moving quickly up the ladder in the prosecutor's office. He was good at his job, had a no-nonsense attitude and influential friends. But as always, the situation left Jenny on the outside of her son's life.

Ruth's phone remained silent that night.

+++

At the police station, there were questions about prostitution and money laundering. Jenny was booked, fingerprinted, photographed, and provided a handwriting sample when asked. Jenny also had to give blood samples to detect possible venereal disease. Jenny told herself, *don't answer questions. Ask for a cigarette. Use tough language. Don't let them bully you. Ask for a lawyer!*

The investigators attempted persuasion via good cop-bad cop tactics.

"One way or another, we'll get the truth," the bad cop snarled. Jenny wanted to cry.

Then she thought, *Maggie, Ruby, Dockett, and Momma Clara wouldn't cry. They'd tell them all to go to hell—well, not Momma Clara.* This brought a smile to her face. A reporter outside the interrogation room window took her picture.

The arraignment took place that afternoon, in a packed courtroom. Jenny could not understand most of the courtroom language. *I just want out of here.* Bail was denied due to the charges and possible flight risk. Jenny entered a non-guilty plea. The judge requested a grand jury hearing, based on the murder and human trafficking charges.

+++

When Ruth saw the paper, she felt sick. On the front page was a picture of Jenny, all in red, smoking a cigarette and smiling. The caption read: *Red Siren remains cool in the hot seat.*

Ruth believed in fate. Without planning it, she'd become Jenny Stone's friend and had fallen in love with her, and together they loved a wonderful little boy.

Now her friend, and the woman she secretly loved, needed her help. But how to get in and see her?

The answer was Jet. *Who else could get me into that jail? Only the most influential prosecutor in New York.*

She hurried to see Jet. Since everyone knew her, she was ushered directly into his stylish office.

"Aunt Ruth," Jet said. "Before you start, Amy and I want you to have dinner with us tomorrow night. Now, aren't you sorry you came down here to nag me about staying away?"

"Well, Mr. Smart-Aleck Prosecutor," Ruth said as they hugged, "that has nothing to do with my visit. My last assignment for my psychology class requires an interview with someone who has a criminal history. I read about a woman who's in this jail. That would help me finally finish that class."

"You want to talk to her, get her side of the story? Really, Aunt Ruth! Anyway, she's not my case. I assigned Jason to that one—it's probably open and shut, with so much evidence. Prostitutes and mobsters get into it all the time."

"Well," Ruth pushed on, "we're about the same age, so I thought it would be easier to talk to her."

"Easier, maybe," Jet allowed, "but still useless.

Aunt Ruth, this is just another woman with little education, jobless, who sold herself into prostitution and played with the bad guys."

"Can't you at least make a phone call? It would be so much harder just to show up at a jail somewhere to try to talk to some criminal. At least here, I know I'm safe. She's in a secure cell in the municipal building."

"All right! All right! I'll try to arrange a meeting. You won't be able to talk about her crime or the investigation. We'll tell her this in advance. Also, I want to know what goes on, if it can help our case. Make it fast and promise you'll be careful. I can only protect you so far."

He looked at her sternly. "One more thing. There's a black man down there when a prisoner's in the cell. He keeps the place clean. The guards escort him to and from the jail. Sometimes, he stays overnight if they get busy. He's always shackled. But stay away from him. You'll be escorted to and from her cell."

Ruth waited for what seemed an eternity for Jet to notify the FBI about her visit. After two hours, he granted her permission. She felt jittery, it was difficult to stand.

A guard called Boxer took her downstairs to the cell. As they walked down a dim staircase to the basement, Boxer told Ruth the rules.

Then she heard a noise in the dark corner of the stairwell. It sounded like a growl or groan.

Boxer walked over to the space and said, "Shut up, Jacob, there's company down here."

The dark corner said, "Yes, sir, boss."

They went to a door with a tiny window in the top. Another guard sat outside the door.

"Okay, lady, when you're ready to leave, just push that buzzer on the wall. The officer will open the door."

He unlocked the door. Ruth stepped inside, and the guard closed the door quickly behind her.

The small cell was dimly lit by a bulb in the nine-foot ceiling. On the cot, her back turned to Ruth, Jenny curled up under a blanket.

Ruth cleared her throat and said softly, "Jenny, Jenny, it's me, Ruth."

The blanket moved, and Jenny turned over. Ruth saw a huge blue mark on Jenny's left cheek.

Ruth went over and almost forgot they were supposed to be strangers. "Oh my God, Jenny, why did you fight them?"

A tear fell on Jenny's cheek. She wiped it away with her hand. "I didn't," she whispered.

"Jenny, this is awful. First, I need to tell you I'm pretending to interview you for a psychology class. We're strangers. Second, I got permission to be here because Jet made a phone call."

Jenny jumped off the cot and grabbed Ruth's shoulder. "Jet! Ruth, you didn't! How could you? On your life, you *swore* you would never tell him!" She collapsed on the cot.

"Jenny, I didn't tell him anything! *He doesn't know who you are.* In fact, another prosecutor has your case; it's not even in Jet's jurisdiction."

Jenny put her hands to her face and then looked up at Ruth. "What's going on? They won't tell me anything. I got so mad, I started screaming at that ugly beast of a guard, and he hit me. Ruth, I have no rights down here. I need answers."

"Jenny," Ruth cautioned, "calm down. They might hear us and make me leave. What are they saying you did?"

Jenny motioned for Ruth to lean closer and whispered, "They think I was involved with the murder of two men. The police had search and arrest warrants."

Ruth gasped and sat down hard on the cot, crowding Jenny in the narrow space. "What the hell! Jenny, that's crazy! That can't be true!"

"Which part, Ruth? The part about the murders or the part about being crazy? Remember, you haven't been around much lately. You have a wedding to prepare for."

"Okay, I hear you trying to make me angry, but it's not working, mother of the groom." She reached over and held one of Jenny's hands. "I love you Jenny, and your son is one lucky young man. Now, I need information about this mess. Let's see what I can find out. I'll come back tomorrow, and Jenny, *please* don't talk to that guard, he's trouble."

"Ruth," Jenny lowered her voice. "when you come back, help me get cleaned up. Until then, I'll pretend to sleep. My bathroom is over there, and the plumbing is broken." She pointed to a dirty toilet with the seat broken and a sink with one rusted faucet.

Ruth grimaced. "What? This isn't really a cell. You're in some kind of secure room, I think.

Oh, Jenny, I'm so sorry. Tomorrow, we'll know more and get things cleared up. I'm going to ring the buzzer. We can't hug. That window is high, but they still may be watching, and we can't afford the risk. Promise me, Jenny, that you'll hold on, as always."

"I promise," Jenny said, wishing time would speed up. Her mind was hovering on the brink of insanity. Five minutes in this hellhole was an eternity. She steeled herself to hold on, for Ruth.

The next day Ruth learned a great deal from the paper. According to the morning news, Jenny was already guilty.

Well, the one thing she *could* do was get back in to see Jenny, lying to Jet about following this prisoner's attitude for my report. Yes, he could arrange it. She managed to hide the newspaper under her blouse.

Once again, the Beast, the name Jenny and Ruth called him behind his back, was on duty. Ruth put her purse on the table.

The Beast spoke, "I got a call. They said you were coming in. Heard you're a nurse."

"Yes, I am," Ruth answered politely. Being the aunt of the DA's lead prosecutor made things tolerable for her. Being a nurse, as well, seemed to change his attitude a little.

"Well," he continued, "when you're down there, you may want to take a look at her. She's been in bed all day."

"Don't you have a doctor available?" Ruth asked.

"Sure," he snorted, "but I'm not bothering him, just 'cause that whore's trying to be lazy."

Ruth kept quiet as they walked down to the basement. The Beast kept talking about street women and drugs. He seemed to have firsthand knowledge about these women. Following protocol, another guard stood or sat outside Jenny's cell, sleeping or reading.

From the start, Ruth simply ignored the Beast, then a noise around the corner caught her attention. She saw the black man, wearing denim overalls with an old gray long sleeve shirt, no shoes, and heavy chains on his feet. He was mopping the floor. The Beast kicked the mop bucket and turned it over. As an afterthought, he hit the man with his billy club and said, "Clean it up."

The black man hobbled over to where the bucket lay and said, "Yes, sir."

The Beast looked over and remarked "Yes, sir, what?"

"Yes, sir, Mr. Boss," he answered.

Ruth bit her lip, trying to remain focused on her task. The Beast ordered the other officer to unlock the door. The odor was so offensive she gagged.

Jenny was sitting on the bed, her back against the wall, knees up under her chin. She had a blanket wrapped around her and was rocking back and forth.

"Jenny," Ruth said, with a quick glance at the closed door. "In a few minutes, your attorney will be here. Read this quickly. I need to know anything I can do to help."

Ruth watched Jenny's face as she read the story. "What the devil is going on, Ruth? What is all this?"

"Jenny, were you *there*? I know you didn't kill anyone, but *were you there*?"

Jenny told Ruth everything she could remember, just the way it happened. A noise outside the room made them stop talking. The door opened, and a woman in a business suit put her hand to her nose and mouth and stumbled out. She never looked at Ruth or Jenny.

Outside the door, she turned to the Beast without blinking an eye. "Get this woman a female officer. *Now.*"

Within fifteen minutes, a short, overweight woman in uniform unlocked the door and came in.

"I'm Linda. They never told me a woman was down here. Let's get you to the showers. I'll get a prison dress for you and personal hygiene products. Your toilet needs cleaning. Big Jacob will do that while you clean up." She looked at Ruth. "Are you a friend?"

"Yes, yes, I am," Ruth replied. "Can I do anything to help?"

"You'll need to leave because we're going down the hall." Linda opened the cell door. She looked at Jenny. "Do you need your friend to take care of anything for you?"

Before Jenny could speak, Linda continued, "The word around the department is, you got yourself a very nice lawyer. She's young, but I hear she's smart, and the men here will behave around you. She's respected, 'cause she's going to marry that big-time prosecutor in the DA's office."

"What?" Ruth asked. "What--I mean..." Ruth did not finish the sentence but exchanged a knowing look with Jenny. "Who are you talking about?" Ruth asked.

"Your friend's public-defense attorney is Miss Amy Collins. She's the fiancée of Mr. Jet Thomas. So, now that she's on the case, at least your friend will be treated right," Linda said.

Ruth and Jenny looked at each other with joy. She gave Jenny a hug, and without hesitation said, "Actually, we just met. I'm interviewing her for a college-class project."

"Right," Linda said. "Let's go before we *all* get sick in here." She left the door open and hollered, "Jacob, get this toilet cleaned and fixed while we're gone."

The next afternoon, Ruth returned. The cell had been cleaned and the bed changed. The terrible odor was gone. Jenny was showered, shampooed, and wore a prison dress.

"Well, you've been busy," Ruth said. She sat down on a chair that had not been there yesterday.

+++

The grand jury met with sixteen randomly-selected individuals to listen to the evidence. Neither Jenny nor her lawyer were present. Of course, the prosecution presented the barest amount of evidence necessary to secure an indictment.

After hearing from the grand jury, the judge handed down an indictment and moved for a trial as soon as possible. He spoke in a 'let's-get-on-with-it' tone.

"All motions and other matters by both sides should be disposed of by September 11th. The trial is on the docket for September 23. Jury selection will begin in one week. A copy of all proceedings will be forwarded to the client and her lawyer."

+++

"Well, I'm a busy murderer," Jenny said cynically. "According to my court-appointed attorney, my chance of proving my innocence to *any* of the charges is almost impossible. She wants me to accept a plea bargain. And also, why do I qualify for a free attorney? I own an entire damn apartment building."

"Dear God in heaven! What are you even talking about?" exclaimed Ruth. "What evidence do they have? What's a plea whatever-you-said?"

"Well, my lawyer says, if I plead guilty to human trafficking, one count of first-degree murder, and turn state's evidence against the mob, the state agrees to recommend a life sentence instead of the death penalty. I refuse to discuss this option. I will not take my life and give my son death," Jenny said in an unwavering voice.

She paced the floor. "At this point, my life and death are in the hands of the mob. I could have taken a deal. With what I know, trouble would still find me. Marty was involved in the human trafficking, all those years ago. Johnny knew something that caused his death *and mine*, as far as they know.

I never went back to our apartment, after he was killed, you know. I was afraid they would find out where we lived. Sure, I ran away, but running away is not the same as being free.

"My life mattered once to a little boy. Now my death will matter to a young man.

"Ruth, I know I'm in a lot of trouble. I'm in way over my head. I'm trying to put pieces together. When Amy comes tomorrow, I'll know more.

Speedy and Charlie went after those guys at the warehouse, and I guess the fight got out of hand. The police are trying to find them. I described them to Amy and told her they worked at the club.

Now, when you come back, bring my comb and lipstick. It'll be okay. Amy will leave word at the desk. She and my son are a perfect match; independent, hard-working, and good values. There'll be plenty of love and admiration to strengthen and support each other."

"Well, I must say," Ruth said, surprised, "I like the sound of that."

Jenny stood in the center of the cell, exuding calm and focus. "Ruth, I've decided to get tough. The weak would never survive this. I'll give Amy just enough information to get me out of here and I have a package for you to mail to Jet." We have a wedding to plan. So, get ready for Jenny Stone, the Red Siren."

+++

It was over a week later that Amy met with Jenny for the second time. The trial date remained on the court calendar for September 23, thirty days away.

Amy sat across from Jenny and studied her for a moment, then removed some papers from her briefcase. "You better take a look at this material," Amy said. She sounded oddly concerned. "The FBI searched those boxes they removed from your house. This is a copy of some of the information."

Jenny read the names of corrupt police and politicians and money transfers from the underage international prostitution business, along with other businesses paying for protection. She gave a sudden gasp.

Most of the records had her signature as the person receiving the property. And if that wasn't enough proof, Amy also had the photograph of Jenny talking to a group of Hong Kong girls as they stood together at the New York airport. *How did they get that picture?*

"Miss Stone, the FBI is handling this case, and the contents of the boxes in your apartment tie you directly to the Hong Kong connection. The District Attorney's office will take over this case. It's already caught the attention of Jet Thomas. He's the prosecutor that mobsters hate and fear. I promise you; he rarely loses a case.

Now, I need to give you a recommendation from my office. I have to remove myself as your attorney. If Jet Thomas is the prosecutor, I cannot be your defense attorney." She actually blushed a little. "I have a personal relationship with Mr. Thomas, so it would be a huge conflict of interest.

Also, I checked with the bank as you instructed about your apartment building. They said it was on the books to be auctioned, due to non-payment of the account for six months. They sent you notices but received no reply."

Jenny remained silent. *Roger had obviously kept the money.*

"Miss Stone, do you understand what I just said?"

"Yes, honey. I may be an accused criminal, but I'm not deaf. Someone sold me down the river. I thought I was going to hell, and now I'm sure of it."

"Miss Stone, listen. Human trafficking is an *international* crime."

"No, *you* listen," Jenny instructed, her temper rising. "Before you go, tell me who were the men killed?"

"One was a bodyguard, Stacy Dillon. The other was the oldest known mob boss on the East side, a big fish, Marty Rigeno. He ran the entertainment side.

"The FBI has been trying to connect Tony Salvadore to Marty Rigeno, and now, you're the connection. The two men you refer to as Speedy and Charlie have turned state's evidence. They contend that you asked them to go with you to that warehouse. Upon entering, you shot Marty Rigeno. Speedy stated that he shot the bodyguard in self-defense."

"Get the hell out!" Jenny screamed. "And take that damn photograph with you!" At that point a curtain came down over the life of Jenny Stone.

Amy rang the buzzer.

"Please Jenny, work with the FBI. They might get you a plea bargain."

"Are you deaf, Miss Collins?" Jenny shouted. "Get out of my sight!" Jenny fell on her bed and turned her face to the wall.

Upon leaving the cell, Amy felt a chill in her body and a sadness in her mind. *This woman needs a miracle to stay alive.*

CHAPTER NINETEEN

The Betrayal

Ruth left early for the jail and missed the call from Jet regarding recent information about the prisoner.

+++

Once the cell door closed, Ruth was immediately set upon by Jenny.

"Ruth, get away from me, leave me alone! Forget that you know me! Don't ever come near me again!"

Ruth remained still. Jenny was in a manic state. She had to talk to her as quietly as possible. "What's going on, Jenny? What's happened?"

Jenny paced the cell, wringing her hands, shivering. "Damn it, Ruth! *Johnny's killer is gonna get me killed.* That son of a bitch Marty *was one of the murdered men.* He *was the East side mob boss.* Marty and Tony were rivals; they each wanted to own the prostitution business.

Do you even understand, Ruth? Tony is alive. He needs me *and everyone connected with me,* dead. It's his only hope for survival. Murder is ugly, and according to the papers, my hands have blood money on them.

If I expose Jet, *you* would be exposed, too. I've been double-crossed, and Ruth, if you keep coming here, *they will get to you!* My death matters enormously to the mob. I've been thinking hard. Trouble would follow me and anyone I trust and love. There's too much exposure here for Tony. He does things his way, and *no one* will be spared from his violence.

He set up Marty's death. I just happened to be in the wrong place at the wrong time. They used me without even knowing my connection to Marty. Why Ruth, why?

I'm really glad he's dead, after what he did to me. But I can't let *anyone* know my connection to him.

Tony's now in complete control. I have nothing to lose by telling everything I know about Tony's business, and it'll be the truth.

I knew most of what Tony was doing, but he never considered me a threat. I'm not some little innocent freak, anymore. I may go down, but I'm going to take him with me."

Ruth looked at Jenny with a great hurt in her heart. "Jenny, you can trust me. You've always known that. Please, tell me something I can do to help you."

Jenny kept pacing.

"Did you hear me?" Ruth asked. She took deep breaths, trying to calm down. Jenny's jitters were starting to terrify her.

"Okay, Ruth, let's see if you're the smart one. We already know who's the dumb ass. Now, listen, I wrote a note to Momma Clara. I'm worried about her. This note tells her to go to her sister's home in Cleveland, *now*. She needs to get out of Tony's house as fast as possible.

"You call the apartment lobby. Roger will answer. Don't talk to *anyone*, except Roger. Set up a meeting and give him the note. Tell him to give the note to Clara, the cook. Make sure he understands *no one else* is to read this note.

Momma Clara has nothing to do with this. It'll kill her if the FBI starts questioning her. By the way, Roger has been taking my rent money and not paying the bank. Amy told me. The apartment income doesn't exist, anymore. Keep this information to yourself. Don't let him know. He'll be taken care of when I'm ready."

"You're frightening me, Jenny," Ruth said. Her voice trembled.

"Listen, Ruth, this is a crazy, mixed-up mess. Just do what I say, will you?" She handed Ruth a sealed envelope.

"Yes, all right," Ruth agreed. "I'll be back. Don't give up, Jenny. We've been through too much…"

+++

Ruth stopped in mid-sentence. She felt an overwhelming sense of doom. She put the note inside her blouse, leaned over and pushed the guard button.

As soon as Ruth arrived home, she telephoned Roger. He agreed to meet her in a tavern on Banks Street.

Ruth remained cautious but determined. Roger knew Ruth had been Jenny's nurse in the hospital.

"Roger, this is from Jenny. I'm continuing to follow her as long as possible for a case study for my class, though I never expected to follow a patient to a jail cell."

"How is she doing, Miss Ruth?" Roger asked.

"I really don't know. She doesn't have much to say. Will you give this note to Clara? Jenny said not to give it to anyone else."

"Did she say what's in it, Miss Ruth? I could just call Clara and tell her, I guess."

"No! Don't do that. The envelope is sealed, and I have no idea of the contents. I think you and I need to stay out of it."

"Well, okay, if that's what she said; it goes straight to Clara, then. And Miss Ruth, when you see Miss Jenny again, tell her I'm looking after the place for her and still collecting her rents."

"I will, Roger, and I'm sure she appreciates what you're doing." *You evil fool.* Ruth picked up her purse, handed the envelope to Roger and left.

Roger arrived the next morning at Tony's house. He rang the doorbell twice and waited.

+++

Clara sat at the kitchen table alone. Sometimes, she still talked aloud to Ben, forgetting he was in the state nursing home. She sang her hymns, went to church, read her bible, and said her prayers.

Tony had hired a company to take care of the garden and two girls to help clean and shop for groceries.

Clara turned her head, got up from the table. *What was that noise? It's the doorbell. It could be Jenny and Ruth. No, they always called to make sure I was alone before visiting.*

Clara opened the door and peered out. The man turned around. He was almost at the end of the porch. Clara watched him and frowned. She noticed an envelope in his hand.

"What you want, Mister?" she asked.

He was looking at the porch floor. Clara kept the screen door between them.

The man looked into the woman's face and with a kind voice said, "My name is Roger. I'm a friend of Jenny's. I have a note for Clara, the cook."

Clara's heart leaped with hope, but she tried to remain calm. "Well, I'm Clara, the cook. You can leave it with me."

Roger knew she was Clara. He recognized her from the description he'd been given.

Clara opened the screen door and stuck her hand out. Roger put the envelope in it and asked, "Now, you want me to read it to you?"

"Oh! No, never mind. I can read anything my Jenny wants me to read." Clara shut the door, kissed the envelope and went hurriedly to the kitchen.

"Glory be. Lordy, Lordy, my prayers been answered." Locating her glasses, she sat down in the old rocking chair and read the note: *Momma Clara, I need to see you. I have a favorite place to show you and something important to tell you. Please meet me Tuesday evening at eight o'clock at the McDaniel's Apartment Building. Take the elevator to the tenth floor, apartment 1010. Momma Clara, please bring some of your biscuits. Love you, Jenny."*

Clara read it over and over. Speaking aloud to no one, she said, "Well, I suppose Mr. Tony's driver won't mind taking me. Now, what has that child gone and done? Got herself some fancy place. Maybe that girl is gonna get married; well, not without her Momma! Now, I need to tell her I'm too old to care for little ones. I could help out maybe a little.

"Let's see, Tuesday. Now, what is today? Where's the calendar?" Clara looked up the pages. "Today is Saturday. Enough time to clean this house, cook the biscuits for my baby and leave Mr. Tony a note. Maybe, on the way back, I'll talk that driver into stopping at the nursing home. Old Ben will be surprised. Lord, I hope I don't go and give him a heart attack."

Clara laughed. She had not felt this good in a long time. "Tomorrow, I'm going to church and thank Jesus for my blessings. Now, my 'bad' days are gonna be my 'good' days."

Charlie arrived at Tony's house at seven o'clock as Clara had requested. He blew the horn. Out came the black woman in her best church clothes, with a hat on her head.

He remained in the car. Clara got in the back. He said, "Something smells like homemade biscuits. Can I have a taste?"

"No sir, you just drive this car to the McDaniel Building. Do you know where that is?"

"Yes ma'am, I do." After about thirty minutes, the car pulled up at the curb of a tall building that looked almost empty. A few lights shone through dirty windows.

"You sure this is the place?" Clara asked doubtfully, afraid to get out of the car.

"This is it," Charlie reassured her. "I guess your friend lives in one of the apartments. Well, get out lady," Charlie added. "Call a cab to take you home."

Clara got out and walked inside. *Lord, the light is so dim, these old eyes having trouble seeing the numbers.* Then she remembered. *Take the elevator to the tenth floor.* Across the hall, she saw the elevator doors and pushed one of the buttons. Doors opened, and Clara felt a sense of relief. She pushed the tenth-floor button.

The biscuits' aroma brought comfort and created a warm, loving sensation, but she felt a little dizzy from the elevator ride. It would be nice to sit at the table with her baby and eat my biscuits, like old times.

The elevator ground to a halt, doors opened. There was no time to be lost. Clara dismissed negative thoughts. She hugged the basket against her chest, looking carefully for apartment 1010. There it was. She breathed deeply and knocked.

Immediately, the door opened. There stood two white men. Clara remembered the short, bald guy from meetings at Tony's house. She had never seen the tall man before.

"Well, hello," said the bald guy, standing a little too close. "You must be Clara."

"Yes, I am, and I did not come here to see you. I came to see my Jenny and you better tell her I'm here."

"Now, now," said the other soothingly. "Don't go getting upset. Jenny is waiting for you on the balcony. We're here to protect her."

"Protect her from what, men like you? I can see I need to talk with that girl and put a little sense in her head."

The two men slid the balcony doors open. Clara went straight onto the balcony. She looked everywhere, but she didn't see Jenny. Clara said quietly, "Jenny, baby, you out here? Momma Clara is here, just like you wanted. Don't be afraid."

At that moment, the two men started laughing. They walked toward Clara, blocking her from going inside. "Guess she didn't show up," the bald man said.

"Get outa my way, you no-good liars. I'm gonna find my baby."

The two men took Clara by the arms and pushed her against the old wooden balcony rail. Tony told them to scare her and instruct her never to talk to anyone about Jenny. She was never to go back to his house.

"You're wasting your time, Clara," the tall man said. "Tony sent us for you. Jenny is dead, and he never wants to see you again." They forced her to look down onto the street, so many floors below, and began laughing.

With her back against the rotten balcony, Clara feared they were going to throw her off the balcony. She was too tired to resist, and her heart was breaking, especially with Jenny gone. With one last effort, they pushed her against the rail to scare her, but Clara would not let go of their coats.

"Turn us loose, damn it!" the bald guy shouted. "We're not going to hurt you. You'll get us all killed!"

As they all struggled, the entire rotten wood rail suddenly broke away. All three fell straight down to the street with the broken boards.

It was nine o'clock on a lovely night. Clara lay on the cold pavement. The two men had died on impact, when they hit the ground. She had not, but no one had come to help her. She could not move, and it was too getting too hard to breathe.

She looked up to her heaven and saw a dazzling star blinking. Clara smiled and let go.

CHAPTER TWENTY

The Four Words

The guards protested bitterly, predicting dire consequences if the convict continued to have visitors and outside walking privileges. No one would say what they thought, that a major mob connection was downstairs, inviting danger for all of them, continually.

Jet cleared the air at the morning roll call. "What you're most afraid of *will not happen*. This situation will prove that we commit ourselves not just to the safety of our employees, but also to the public we serve."

Ruth followed Jet's instructions. She wore her nurse's uniform for each visit. She carried paper and pen with her, and sometimes brought the officers home-made cake and cookies.

Upon entering the cell one day, Ruth said quietly, "Jenny, why the stone face? What's wrong?"

"My new smart-ass lawyer, Robert Harrison," Jenny said, as she looked at Ruth, her face empty, "told me that Charlie and Speedy confessed to going with me the night of the murders. They turned state's evidence and described the murder scene. They said I was drunk and crazy when I killed Marty. Speedy confessed to killing the bodyguard in self-defense.

A police undercover informant working at the club signed an affidavit describing my involvement with the mob, including storing property like counterfeit bank notes and stolen license plates.

The assistant prosecutor presented circumstantial evidence that I was identified at the crime scene on Cedar Street and refused to stop for a blue light and sirens. They didn't see anyone else in the car.

Although Tony Salvadore is on the FBI's wanted list for questioning, they haven't uncovered any evidence to incriminate him. The smart-ass made it clear that more evidence was being made available by the FBI.

The state collected concrete evidence against me: There are boxes of documents signed for by me, two confessions directly placing me at the murder scene, and my fingerprints on the murder weapon and car.

They have a clear and neat case. If I agree to assist the FBI with the Tony Salvadore investigation, things could be made easier for me. You know, like maybe life in prison instead of the gas chamber.

Ruth, Tony wants me dead. After Baxter's death, we both played each other for our own gains. I accumulated a nice bank account, and he knew I was leaving. I became a mob member out of stupidity, then I used Tony's connections as a way out. When I die, the last person who could tie Tony to anything illegal will be gone."

Ruth didn't say anything. She couldn't think of anything that might help.

+++

As the days passed, so did the meetings with her attorney. Jenny treated the guy with more respect after she read some of the information he planned to use in her defense.

He mentioned Doris Green, a waitress at the Blue Moon. He said she would testify that Jenny left that night with Charlie and Speedy. She saw Jenny get into their back seat and knew she wasn't intoxicated, just exhausted.

Jenny's thoughts wandered about her past choices and decisions that now led to this cliff of a grave. Death or illness is never accidental. It's always caused by the spirit or human energy.

+++

The trial began with a flood of front-page news stories: some true, some lurid and unproven, though the public didn't care and ate it all up. However, they all played up Jet Thomas as honest, brave and a huge enemy of the mob.

Jenny Stone was made out to be an impulsive person whose association with the mob was willful. They said she had no respect for those she hurt, that she did whatever she had to, for wealth and power.

The papers continued the theme of The Red Siren. Most photographs of Jenny showed her wearing red and smiling. Naturally, these were chosen from the boxes of similar photographs found in her apartment.

+++

Jenny's lonely days were spent preparing information for Jet to investigate after her death. She loved her son, and she didn't have time to be afraid.

She kept some remaining control over her life through the clothes she asked Ruth to bring for her court appearances. For the trial, Ruth brought Jenny a simple barber pole-striped shirt with a wing collar, Gibson-girl sleeves, flared cuffs, and a grey button skirt.

Her shoes were two-inch flannel accent pumps--gray flannel accented with black calf suede.

The case had reached federal levels, and Jet Thomas was leading the DA's case, as Amy had told Jenny long ago. Jenny couldn't wait to watch Jet in the courtroom, to listen to his voice, to drink in his essence, to salve her long years of loneliness by having him close by, even as he made the case against her.

She wanted more than ever to be in charge of stopping her runaway life, if only to make Jet proud at the very end of it.

I cannot go back and start my life over, but I can determine the ending. My life will not have been pointless. The destruction of Tony Salvadore is something that's in my hands. I can expose him with concrete evidence, and Jet can have all the credit. It will be my final gift to him.

+++

At 10:30 a.m. on September 23, Jenny followed the guards outside to a transport van. Dark clouds covered a wet sky.

Inside the courtroom she sat beside her attorney, Robert. He was a good-looking young man with sandy hair, mustache, short beard and a slender build, wearing a grey suit and silk tie. She saw Ruth slip through the door into the rear of the courtroom.

She drummed her fingers on the table, watched and waited for one person. Then he entered and sat behind the prosecutor's table, conveniently located on the side of the room closest to the jury box.

He looked directly at her. Jenny smiled and said quietly to herself, "So Jet, my darling, you're in charge now."

Her smile disconcerted him. He looked down at his papers on the table.

The bailiff instructed, "All rise for the Honorable Judge Martin Anderson and remain standing until the jury is seated."

Jenny watched seven men and five women take seats. *Do they want to believe I'm innocent? They have such hollow looks and condescending smiles. Are they going to steal my life?*

As she studied their faces, Jenny knew she had already been tried and convicted in their minds. It didn't make the slightest difference what anyone said. They already presumed she was guilty; why else would Jet Thomas be trying the case?

Tony might also have found a way to stack the jury. Either way, throughout her life, not many people were willing to give her the benefit of the doubt. She knew what their looks at her indicated.

To make matters worse, Doris Green, the waitress from the Blue Moon, had been admitted to Cannon Mental Hospital after a drug overdose. *Very convenient, Tony. Another mob hit.*

The bailiff announced, "The People versus Jenny Stone."

The prosecution began its opening statement to the judge and jury.

Jet spoke, his voice chilled steel. "Police accounts show the stolen car and the murder weapon had the defendant's fingerprints on them. The police report states they chased the defendant using their siren and blue lights, but she refused to stop. They didn't see anyone else in the car as it sped out of sight. An officer found the abandoned vehicle in an alley. The desk clerk at Miss Stone's apartment building stated he heard someone using the key to the building door at approximately five a.m., and opened his door, just in time to see Miss Stone enter."

Jet continued, "Her motive was money and power. The murdered men were Marty Rigeno, a crime boss from Chicago, and his bodyguard. The defendant has been working with Tony Salvadore's eastside operation to eliminate Marty Rigeno's part of the trafficking profits. The court has sworn affidavits from employees of the Blue Moon Club.

"We can also connect Miss Stone to the Hong Kong underage human sex trafficking ring."

"Young people are suffering as sex slaves, and two men have been murdered in a heinous and cruel manner. There are no mitigating circumstances here. If a person violates the law, he is to be prosecuted to the fullest extent, and there are no exceptions! I urge you, ladies and gentlemen, in this case, do justice, do right."

Jet thanked the jury. "That concludes my opening statement, Your Honor."

+++

Jenny had to admit: Robert delivered quite a case. He made clear that she had no previous criminal record, nor had she even been *suspected* of committing a crime. She was employed by Tony Salvadore only to keep records and run errands.

He pounded on the jury-box rail and pleaded with the jury to place themselves in the defendant's position: She attended school full-time, sang at the Blue Moon Club, managed an apartment building, and performed her job as directed by Tony Salvadore. She wasn't romantically involved with any men, nor did she have a drug problem.

Evidence would prove that Tony Salvadore's lawyer set up the human-trafficking business through the private non-profit name Relocation for Refugees Foundation. Miss Stone had no reason to doubt the legalities.

The attorney thanked the jury. "That concludes my opening statement, Your Honor."

+++

The ordeal began.

Jet had the police officers and Grady Rogers take the stand under oath and acknowledge their statements. He presented the murder weapon.

Speedy (Carl Mullis) was sworn in. He looked over at Jenny through his big glasses. Jenny shot him a hard, cold stare. He quickly lowered his head.

He said, "Miss Stone and me went into the warehouse. She shot Mr. Rigeno, and I had to shoot the bodyguard in self-defense. She ran out the building and left.

"Charlie was waiting outside. We caught a cab and slept at the club. We told nobody nothing."

Jet called the medical examiner to the stand. During his testimony, he showed enlarged pictures of the victims. The body of Marty Rigeno was shattered with bullet holes. The bullets proved a positive match to the gun found in the car. Some of the jurors refused to look at the pictures.

Throughout the trial, Jenny's mind battled with her memories. *My life has been a contest: light against darkness, hope against despair. How do I stop the ticking clock?*

Cross-examination of all witnesses by prosecution and defense continued for over four hours. Both presented their closing arguments.

Jenny claimed one brief chilling moment in that courtroom. During her cross-examination by Jet, she looked into Johnny's beautiful blue eyes. Jet placed his arm on the witness stand rail while addressing the jury. *Touch him. Touch him,* her body screamed. She locked her hands together and squeezed helpful pain. Her gut exploded. She tasted the bile in her mouth and forced it down, thankful that she had not eaten. Somebody called her name.

"Miss Stone, answer the question," ordered the Judge. She remained silent, *what question.*

Jet was instructed to repeat the question.

"Did you know Tony Salvadore was a mob boss?"

"Yes, but..."

"Just answer the question, yes or no, Miss Stone."

"Yes." *I knew something about the mob, but my God, I never knew I was hurting anyone. Every time something happened, I tried to explain it away. Now I know I was a fool.* These thoughts fostered her statement.

She told the truth and spoke freely of her involvement in club activities as an employee and her version of the night of the murder.

Marty is dead, and so is my past. I pray they have enough gossip; that my life before Tony is not important to them. Jet will know, finally, in time.

The jury appeared restless. They wanted to be somewhere else. The human-trafficking discussions were painful; two women on the jury reached for tissues.

The judge instructed the jury, "Carry out your duties, taking into account the arguments from the prosecutors, the defense attorney and the routine and drawn instructions." The twelve selected jurors were ushered out of the courtroom to begin deliberations.

+++

The jury reached a verdict in less than five hours. Jenny was transported back to the courtroom from her cell. She had not seen Ruth.

The foreman handed the piece of paper to the judge.

Judge Anderson looked at Jenny. "Will the defendant please rise?"

Jenny stared straight ahead, as each charge was read by the clerk of court. Jenny's attorney shifted beside her; his hands clenched into fists. She reached over and put one hand over his. She felt close to fainting.

The jury found Jenny guilty on all counts.

The judge let out a deep breath. "On behalf of the state of New York, the defendant, Jenny Stone, has been tried by a jury of her peers and found guilty of all charges. Sentencing will be imposed on September 30, 1958. A pre-sentencing report and any additional information must be received by September 26."

Robert made an immediate post-trial motion, asking the judge to override the jury and either grant a new trial or order the defendant acquitted.

The judge denied the motion.

"This court stands adjourned," said the bailiff.

+++

Later that day, Jenny sat on her cot, emotionally exhausted. Jacob stood on the cold floor under the window of the door. "Jenny, do you want to hear some more verses?"

Jenny heard Jacob talking to her but didn't have the strength to respond. She knew he had memorized the Bible from cover to cover. Often, the two repeated verses together.

"Please answer me, Jenny," he pleaded.

"I am not here, Jacob. I'm in a place of peace," came Jenny's soft voice.

"Is it pretty where you are, Jenny?"

"Oh, Jacob, I close my eyes and remember the spirit of someone who loved me."

"I know that place, Jenny. I been there, too," Jacob said in a faraway voice.

He stood silent, then started humming *Amazing Grace*.

Jenny closed her eyes. Her restless mind found Johnny. *They're right: I should have known what was going on. I chose to overlook the truth. But knowing I've tried, in my own way, to protect my loved ones, makes surrendering my life easier.*

+++

Her days were spent talking to Robert, Jacob, and Ruth. The female prison guard, Linda, came each day to walk with Jenny outside for an hour, and they had some good talks. In another time and another place, they could have been friends. Linda told Jenny there would be no more walks after the sentencing.

Jenny spent most of her time in deep thought. No judge or member of the jury would go against the mob: the risk was too great. *I accept the heavy burden of guilt, knowing my decisions were devastating. I am trapped, and it hurts.*

Sentencing took place one week after the trial. The moment Judge Anderson pronounced the sentence of execution, Jenny knew the rest of her life would be agony.

+++

Jenny's execution by gas was scheduled on Tuesday, October 21, at 6 a.m. Apparently, this was to be a hush-hush execution with limited press. The judge had given the harshest possible punishment. Jenny knew the mob was really in charge of the sentencing. She remembered having seen Judge Anderson in the Blue Moon several times.

Ruth brought the paper every day. Jet was either on the front page or somewhere else inside. Jenny searched each page every day as the columnists speculated about his political future. The last headline read: Jet considers a trip to Washington. *Yes, I gave the halo to my son.*

"My son," Jenny murmured, unaware of her young lawyer's presence.

"What did you say?" Robert asked.

Jenny shook her head. "Just thinking out loud."

"Well," Robert responded, "I'm going to meet with the Governor tomorrow, Miss Stone. I've filed a notice of appeal."

"Robert, you're smart, and you've probably guessed that I process a great deal of information. We have no winning scenario.

You may wonder why I keep secrets that would save my life, and I'll be honest with you. More important lives than mine will benefit from my death. Saving me is a gift I cannot give you."

+++

Jenny was about to close the paper, when she noticed a tiny article regarding three accidental deaths in the fall from a balcony. It was strange--no leads, no information regarding the deceased persons. She started reading aloud.

The bodies of two well-dressed white men and an elderly black woman were found lying on the sidewalk. The cause of death was a fall from the vacant tenth- floor balcony of the condemned McDaniel Building.

Apparently, the three had been eating together. Biscuits were found on the balcony and the street. There was no identification on any of the victims. The incident remains an ongoing investigation.

Jenny read the words over and over.

"Dear God in heaven, not my Momma Clara!" But Jenny knew that somehow, it was.

She put her hand over her mouth to muffle the sobs. "I died today!" she screamed. "I—died--today! I swear, I want to *kill* somebody!" She pounded her fists against the wall. "My God, what

205

Ann Barton

was Momma Clara thinking? Something went wrong. Ruth must find out."

Later, after vomiting until her body was drained, Jenny told Jacob that the black woman who'd died was her Momma Clara. Somehow, they'd used her letter as bait to get to the only person who could be a witness against Tony Salvadore and a character witness for Jenny. The thoughts assaulted her brain endlessly.

Roger worked for Tony. He had to be the mole. He'd not only robbed her; he'd taken away the person who loved her the most.

I'll kill that son of a bitch. He will *pay a price for his deceit! Oh, Momma Clara, I loved you so. I dedicate the rest of my life to you.* Her body crumbled in on itself.

Ruth visited as often as possible but didn't know about Momma Clara until Jenny showed her the paper.

She fidgeted around the cell, unable to sit still. Jenny was so thin and weak.

Two days before the execution, Ruth was unusually late for her visit. During the day, a storm had turned light into darkness. Ruth had never seen so much lightning and such loud bursts of thunder. She thought she might go to the jail later, but a nagging, panicky feeling forced her to drive in the torrential rain to the jail.

Ruth descended the stairs following the guard. He unlocked the door, and Ruth stood in shock.

Jenny was not only fully dressed, but she had also applied make-up. She was full of energy and excitement. Her eyes were bright.

Ruth stood frozen, baffled. "What's going on here?" she asked, tremors in her voice.

Jenny looked straight into Ruth's eyes. "I need to talk to my son. You need to get him down here. I don't give a damn how you do it, but you must."

Ruth spoke loudly over the crashing thunder. "He won't come; it's not right. You have a lawyer."

"Now, listen to me," said a defiant Jenny. "*I need you to do this for me.* My son wants to be governor, *and I can make it happen.* He believes the government should take a firm hand on corruption, no deals, and a safer environment for families. Nobody will help, but I have the answer."

"Jenny, you've lost your mind. I love you, but you'll only hurt Jet's political future by dragging your troubles into his life now."

"Damn you, Ruth, damn you!" Jenny screamed. "He's *my* son. Do you think for one minute that I would ever do anything so stupid?"

"Okay! Calm down! You're confusing me," Ruth said, almost dropping onto the chair. "Now, tell me, how am I supposed to get Jet in here?"

"Tell him I have information, detailed *confidential* information, for his ears only. Ruth, you can be convincing. Tell him in your own way."

"Jenny, you know I love you and I am trying to believe you."

"No, Ruth!" Jenny exclaimed, "I have it! Jet can visit as a noble gesture, saying goodbye to the woman he prosecuted. It'll create even more positive publicity for him!"

Then Jenny warned, "Do not let *anyone* know what you're saying to him and *make sure he understands* to tell *no one* the truth about why he's coming to see me. Also, after he gets down here, he must dismiss the guards."

Ruth was hesitant, but with Jenny becoming almost hysterical in her demands to see Jet, she quietly left the cell.

Two hours passed. "Jenny," Jacob said, "you should pray to calm your nerves."

"My son will be here soon to talk with me. This will be all I need to comfort my soul."

Jacob grinned. "Just listen to you, bragging on your son."

Jenny had told him everything. Jacob and Ruth both knew about Jet, and with them, she could proudly say those words—*my son.*

Jenny paced. Jacob prayed. The storm rattled the windows.

Ruth was giving the performance of a lifetime upstairs. She had patiently waited for two hours. Now, behind the closed doors of his office, she was requesting, not demanding, that Jet listen to the prisoner, Jenny Stone, regarding confidential information for his ears only.

"I am not going to give that woman the benefit of a personal meeting with me. She had her time in court!" Jet yelled at Ruth. "I did try to locate her family, but this selfish woman existed only for the mob. Thank God, there's no child involved."

"Jet, lower your voice." Ruth knew she had to continue pleading Jenny's request. She doubted Jenny had any valuable additional information, but she *did* deserve this moment. *My dear God, what is Jenny going to do? Will she finally tell Jet the truth?*

"Jet," Ruth began, "this is your Aunt Ruth, asking for a big favor. I love you and would never upset your rules, but just visit for a few minutes. I'll stay here. She requested that you come alone. Your officers will accept your explanation that you're doing this to be decent."

"What about that black man? He'll be down there."

"Oh," Ruth said quickly, "Jenny doesn't care about his staying for this."

"Damn it, Aunt Ruth, I *knew* you shouldn't have interviewed that woman! *Damn* that woman! This is just an appeal to *your* need to nurture. Don't you understand Aunt Ruth? She doesn't know the meaning of decency!"

"Watch your tone with me, young man," Ruth spoke hoarsely. She had to turn away to hold back her tears.

Jet walked over to his office door and called to the young brunette behind the desk. "Come in here and keep my aunt company. With this storm, she's a nervous wreck." He motioned for the two policemen to come in as well.

"Believe it or not, gentleman, I'm going to visit our condemned prisoner." He spoke in the most compassionate tone he could muster, while they kidded him about his big heart.

Finally, Jet walked into the hall. *Why did I ever let Aunt Ruth get involved? She's not cut out for this.*

He opened the door to the stairs leading to the cell. The officer on duty was asleep, and Jet thumped him awake and sent him upstairs to get coffee.

All was quiet except for the outside storm. The large room was dim.

Jet knocked on the cell door. "Jenny Stone, I hear you have information for me. I'm not interested in your confession. They don't pay me to waste my time. I'll unlock this door now. I'm warning you, stay away from the door. My officers are upstairs. Do you understand?"

The storm raged outside. There was no response from the cell. He thought she might be asleep or couldn't hear him.

+++

Jenny was almost rigid with tension. She had prepared herself in every detail this morning. With Linda's help, she'd managed to paint her fingernails; now they glowed bright red. Her dress was a soft lavender with a little red collar and red cuffs. Her pumps were lavender with red bows. She had seen the outfit at a bridal shop and bought it at once.

"Miss Stone," Jet repeated louder, "can you hear me? This is the only time I am coming down here, so it's now or never."

"Are you alone?" The voice inside asked.

"Yes. That *is* what you wanted, isn't it?"

"Don't get smart with me," Jenny answered. She was careful to pretend to be the stranger scheduled for execution. "What I want is something you can't give me. Open the door and come in, Mr. Prosecutor."

Jet unlocked the door and stood there. The sight of her left him speechless. She looked different, or maybe he hadn't noticed at the trial that she looked like a movie star.

Jenny broke the silence. Softly, she said, "Why don't you have a seat?" She pointed to the chair and perched on the edge of the cot.

Jet cleared his throat to bring himself back to reality. He sat down, as he was told, and also because he suddenly felt weak. *I should have eaten lunch.* "Let's get on with this information, Miss Stone."

Jenny picked up a small notebook. "I'll explain some things in this notebook, but all the information is in my handwriting. You probably would want it that way. You *are* one for details, aren't you?"

Jet did not answer, but she had his attention; he kept looking directly at her.

Jenny gave names, places, and dates regarding mob activities.

"You need to check out the old McDaniel building as a possible hideout for Tony Salvadore. I know he owns that property and stores records there. You might also find a connection with the mob and the recent deaths of three people at that address." Jenny paused to compose herself, then continued. "Up until now, I've remained quiet about what I know about Tony's affairs. Now, I'll connect the dots for you."

Jenny had kept special documents and all her savings locked away in a safe deposit box, along with records about the Hong Kong girls, Sam's notes from his apartment signed by Tony, with handwritten instructions and many messages, also signed by Tony. She had taken pictures of the mob at Tony's house and compiled a list of corrupt cops and politicians.

After an hour, she said, "Well, Mr. Prosecutor, never mess with a woman who is about to die. My friend Ruth has the key to the deposit box. Ask her and she'll give it to you."

"I'll have to check all this out," Jet said, trying to mask his excitement. He knew he had enough information in his hands—if everything she said was true--to send him straight to Washington. He didn't want to waste time processing the information, especially Tony's secret warehouse.

Jenny knew her time with Jet had run out. She had one task of pure joy up her sleeve. She wanted to touch her son before he left. She told Jacob, "If I could just touch my son, I could at least die with that memory."

Jet stood up. Jenny put her hand out. "How about a good-bye and thank you handshake?"

Jet looked at Jenny. Instead of shaking her hand, he put the key in the door and spoke in a condescending tone. "This information is important. I won't thank you for doing something to ease your conscience." With that, Jet opened and locked the door and started upstairs.

Jenny stood and leaned back against the door. She began to cry, very softly, until she was sobbing in great gulps.

Jacob sat on his chair with tears in his eyes. Then, he listened again. There were footsteps coming down the stairs.

A male voice said, "Miss Stone, step away from the door again. I believe a handshake is appropriate, and I know my aunt would definitely approve."

"Just a moment," Jenny murmured. She quickly wiped her eyes, blew her nose, and smoothed her dress, then stood back.

Jacob took a deep breath. "Thank you, Jesus."

Jenny said in a quiet voice, "Well, open the door. A handshake is difficult through a locked door."

The door opened, and Jenny's son entered once more. Jet looked at this woman again. For the first time, he considered that maybe she had a child somewhere and could have had a different life. But, God, look at what she had chosen! He composed himself. *If the crime fits...*

Jet spoke. "This information will put a stop to some evil and senseless crimes." He held out his hand. Jenny put out her trembling hand toward his.

As their hands met, Jet suddenly felt a sense that he was dreaming. The thunder outside was so loud, he flinched. *He wanted to keep holding this hand.*

For just a second, a vision flashed into his head, of a broken face at a window, that face in a hundred childhood nightmares. He let go abruptly, feeling very uncomfortable, for maybe the first time in his career.

Jenny knew that she must remain strong. "Now, that wasn't so hard, Mr. Prosecutor. Now get out of here, go home, and wash your hands."

Jet slowly turned, opened his mouth to say something, then closed his lips. He opened the door, let it close, and slumped against it. Jenny watched the door close and leaned against it on the inside. After a moment, Jet put the notebook in his coat pocket and went up the stairs.

When he opened his office door, the sergeant said, "Well, that sure was a long good-bye. Everything okay? You look like you seen a ghost."

"You can leave now," Jet said. "I'll drive my aunt home. Get someone to bring her car home."

The storm was letting up as Jet and Ruth left the building. Ruth dared not say a word. Jet did not talk until they were almost home. When he spoke, Ruth held her hand over her heart.

"I'm staying at the office tonight," he blurted out. "I have some information that needs authentication."

She listened quietly. *What has Jenny done? What happened in that cell?*

"But, Jet, you're so overworked now, why don't you let one of the paralegals do the research?"

"No. I won't let this information out of my hands before I'm completely prepared."

"So?" Ruth said slyly. "Did Jenny tell you something important?"

"Aunt Ruth, I love you, and that's why I can't tell you. Miss Stone was hands-on with the mob. She lived in Tony Salvadore's house. Do you know why she waited until now to talk with me? Perhaps we would have considered a plea bargain. No, don't answer my question. She obviously only talked to me to clear her evil conscience."

As soon as Ruth got out of the car, Jet sped away.

Ruth struggled up the front steps, feeling weak. *Oh, Jenny, why didn't you just leave well enough alone?*

The next morning, Thursday, October twentieth, produced another dark sky with a cold northerly wind. Ruth poured a cup of black coffee, not the usual cream and sugar mixture. She usually had toast, but this morning she wasn't hungry.

A little before daybreak tomorrow, my secret love will die. This is for me to bear alone. So many times, recently, she had thought about Jenny, Jet, and the truth. *Why do I have to wait until Jenny is dead?* But she remembered her promise to Jenny: *After her death, let him read the letters. They will contain our lives from meeting his father, Marty's connection, Sam, Momma Clara, Roger, and me.* Sometimes, Ruth thought the secret would kill her.

Getting dressed forced Ruth to think about her seesaw life. Her depression was profound. She tried to weather the moment, however, understanding that preparing a friend for death defies logic.

She and Jet were like strangers. He kept busy with his fact-finding mission and appeared to be on a secret assignment. This made for poor communication.

"I'll be staying at Amy's apartment for a few weeks," he announced. "I need quick access to several important people." Ruth faked a smile in response.

So, on this Wednesday, Ruth drove to the municipal building. *What happened between Jenny and Jet? What could be so urgent?* Deep in thought, she almost missed the last step.

Ruth reached for the cell door, turned, and looked at Jacob. He sat on his cot under the stairwell, reading his Bible.

"Hello, Miss Ruth," Jacob said. The two had become at ease with each other.

"How's she been?" Ruth asked.

"Okay, I guess. The lady helper, Miss Linda, just left and Jenny has been writing ever since. She never ate her breakfast."

Ruth knocked gently on the door, taking deep breaths to calm herself. She rehearsed the detailed instructions the officer had read to Jenny.

+++

"Your cell door will remain unlocked, with the guard standing watch upstairs. Several people with different responsibilities need to come and go. Your attorney will be allowed to visit as necessary. A reporter will try and get a story from a condemned woman. Then, there's a doctor visit, a last-meal order, and the priest at 8 p.m. Your friend must leave at 5 a.m."

+++

She gently knocked again. There was no answer. Ruth opened the cell door and saw Jenny concentrating deeply on her writing. She sat in the chair. This was their routine: Jenny on the cot, Ruth in the chair.

"I'll be in a chair soon enough," Jenny had declared, "so why start now?"

Ruth started to say something, but Jenny held up a finger. "I need to finish. This letter can't wait. I have no tomorrows."

After ten minutes, Jenny folded the papers and placed them in an envelope.

"Ruth, put this in the last box of letters for Jet." With trembling hands, Ruth took the envelope, and then she burst into sobs. Jenny reached over and pulled Ruth onto the cot and hugged her.

"Oh!" Jenny said in a humorous tone, "did I miss something? They're taking you instead of me?"

With this, Ruth blew her nose and managed a weak smile. She was so in love with that voice.

"What is this?" Ruth asked, standing and looking down at the envelope. "My God, Jenny, another letter? What words could you write in it? How am I supposed to deal with Jet after he reads this, and for that manner, after he reads all those letters? What am I going to do when he realizes he sent *his own mother* to the gas chamber? Jenny, can't we just leave well enough alone?"

"What are you saying, Ruth? You're suggesting I remain a secret forever?"

"Jenny, I love you and I love Jet, but I can't help you, and Jet is doing fine without our help."

"Ruth, if it makes you feel better, open and read the letter. I owe you that much, and so much more. The envelope isn't sealed. You see, Ruth, I knew that even now, you'd be thinking about Jet."

"No, Jenny, I didn't mean--"

"Stop it," Jenny said. "You are right, plus I need your opinion about the contents. Now read it. After I die, and Tony Salvadore is dead, my son will have an honest, fearless future, in law or wherever."

> Dear Jet, *by now you have read all my letters. You must know Marty thought that all these years, I was dead. I have tried to clarify with dates and places.*
>
> *Your Aunt Ruth is my dearest and oldest friend. She will help fill in the empty spaces. Early in your life, I was forced to take a different path to keep both of us safe.*
>
> *Your father was a handsome, wonderful man who at age twenty died at the hands of the mob, without a mean or wrong thought in his body. If you want to know what he looked like, just look in the mirror.*
>
> *And, oh, have you ever been loved! I could only love you from a distance, but in spirit, I never left your side. I also managed to get a glimpse of you here and there.*

I am completely innocent of all those unthinkable crimes brought up in court. Being young and ignorant in the ways of crime, I managed to place myself in all the wrong places at the wrong times.

Take the information I gave you and when you have their confessions, you will know my innocence. I have been framed by the mob, and I'm telling you this because when you think of your mother, I want you to, yes, maybe love me.

Jet, I have so much to say to you, so many feelings for you, there is not enough time and room for it all.

I am so proud of my son. I met Amy here in my cell. Let Aunt Ruth tell you about that, and Jet, I really do like her.

So now, my darling, you'll have two angels looking after you, your father and mother. Apparently, we'll be busy. Let Ruth explain why my name is Jenny Stone.

Goodbye my son.

Love, Momma

Ruth read each word with anguish and compassion. She had been standing, but as she finished reading, she almost slid to the floor. She sat on the cot beside Jenny.

"Well," Jenny asked, "do you approve?"

Ruth reached over and the two friends hugged each other for a long time.

"It's a perfect letter," Ruth said. "I just wish it didn't have to be this way."

At that moment came a gentle knock on the door. Linda came in with lunch. She placed the tray on the cot and picked up the untouched breakfast tray.

As she was leaving, she turned. "Jenny, please eat something."

Jenny's head snapped to attention. "Why, Linda, so I can keep up my strength to walk to my death?"

"Later, I'll bring paper for you to write your final meal request." Linda stood a moment, then went out the door.

"Ruth!" Jenny said suddenly. Ruth had been in deep thought and wasn't feeling well. She jumped.

"What is it, Jenny? What's wrong?"

Jenny grabbed Ruth's arms. There was a frantic edge to her voice. "Ruth, get that jail doctor down here to give me something. Tell him if I die or kill myself, it will be on his hands. I feel like worms are crawling under my scalp, down my back and under the skin on my legs. I can feel my heart pounding in my ears. My nerves are crazy and I need a shot of whatever it takes for a person to wait to die. I need help. Don't let him refuse, you understand?" Jenny started screaming and pounding on the walls.

Ruth outweighed Jenny by at least 30 pounds, so she pulled Jenny onto the cot and held her arms tightly at her sides.

"Now, you keep fighting till you're exhausted. You're having a panic attack." Finally, Jenny stopped struggling.

"I'm leaving now. Promise you'll be all right until I get back, Jenny."

"Oh, for God's sake, Ruth, I promise. Go on. I'm going to die and I've chosen no way out. When you come back, bring a clock with you. They took my watch, and I'm getting mixed up about the time of day. Hurry and get that damn doctor."

Ruth closed the door gently, trying to keep Jenny calm, and asked Jacob to please say something to her at different times, to make sure she was all right. Jacob nodded, holding his Bible close to his chest.

+++

At 4 p.m., a knock on the door took Jenny's attention away from her writing. When she looked up, the doctor with his little black bag stood there with Linda.

"Now look, I'll give you something, but you better watch yourself. If you die before they put you in that gas chamber, the DA will have my head. After the execution, I will pronounce you. I don't intend to do it before."

Jenny said, "I'm almost out of your way. Give me something, and get out of here."

Linda opened the door after the doctor finished, and they left. Jenny returned to her note pad. The Thorazine injection stopped her thoughts.

Jenny slept, a deep dreamless sleep.

+++

Ruth drove into her modest neighborhood, parked the car and cried until it hurt to breathe. Then an idea, maybe even a vision, suddenly grabbed her. She went inside, walked down the stairs to the basement, and looked at the locked closet containing all the boxes of letters written by Jenny. She had read most of them at Jenny's request. Now, she placed the final letter in the box.

Ruth shook her head from side to side. She knew she should change clothes, eat something, relax. *Why? So, I can help the love of my life go away forever?*

She went upstairs and paced, her head throbbing. She leaned against the kitchen sink and decided to follow her vision.

She knew Clara's death had forced Jenny into seeking revenge against the mob. This created a death wish for Tony.

Ruth phoned Jet. *What will I say? Oh, I don't care anymore. I'm sick of all the lying and pretending. This is my life, too.*

Jet's secretary answered. She didn't know where Jet was, but she mentioned that he and Amy were going to look at houses for sale. She told Ruth she was leaving the office herself.

"Leave him a note to call me as soon as he comes back," Ruth urged. She knew her voice was shaky, but her decision was made. *Sorry Jenny, I'm not playing this deadly game anymore. The hell with it; I'll take the risk.*

After all, the assistant prosecutor had offered Jenny a safe house for being an informant. Jenny had refused that option.

"No, Jenny had insisted. "Don't ever ask me to do that. The mob sent me to hell once. Never again." Ruth had gone along with Jenny's plan, until now.

Ruth's acceptance of her decision made her feel a little calmer. She ate a sandwich and fell into a disturbing, fitful sleep as soon as her head touched the sofa cushion.

When she sprang awake and looked at the clock, it was midnight. She called Jet's office; no answer. Then she called Amy's apartment. No answer. She called the municipal jail office; they told her Jet wasn't there. Ruth left word to have Jet call her if they saw him.

She quickly showered, dressed and packed the clothes that Jenny had selected to wear: a long-sleeved red dress, flowered, bright-red wedgie open-toed shoes, make-up, red fingernail and toenail polish; Jenny as ever conscious of her appearance, especially her strong color. Hardly able to concentrate, Ruth drove to the jail and arrived at one a.m. Once again, the guard opened the door leading downstairs. He told her the cell door was unlocked. Ruth walked slowly downstairs, holding onto the rail. Linda left the cell with a basin and towels, just as she came in. They exchanged looks; no words were necessary.

Ruth knocked gently and entered. Jenny looked pale and thin on the cot.

They hugged; Ruth could hear Jacob reading Bible verses. Everything was calm, quiet, and almost peaceful.

Ruth spoke first. "I brought your clothes."

"Thanks Ruth. My going-away clothes; I wish they *were* my getting away clothes. Please donate all my pretty clothes and my savings to the Apalachin United Methodist Church in your name. I want the money used for single mothers. Now, let's talk about old times for a little while. You know, when we first met and things were so simple and good."

"Okay by me," Ruth said. "Let's get you dressed while we talk."

They reminisced, cried and laughed.

Ruth kept the pain of her true love and desire restrained within her. They held each other tightly.

Jenny described the priest's visit. She managed a short prayer with him, Jacob, her own preacher, had connections in heaven and would put in a word for her. She knew when she took the last steps, her prayers would be for her son.

Jenny looked stunning when they finished the preparations. With careful make-up, her skin was soft and smooth. She had gone cold turkey on alcohol after her incarceration.

Ruth was always entertained by Jenny's obsession with clothes. Today brought the memories of yesterdays, with no tomorrows, and all hope of the future slipping away.

There were no second chances, no miracles.

+++

After a long afternoon of house hunting, Jet and Amy went out to dinner and a movie. He was prepared to stay at Amy's, then remembered he should call his aunt and tell her not to see the prisoner that night. When he called, there was no answer. He regretted he had distanced himself from her with this whole Jenny Stone ordeal.

"I should be with my aunt tonight," Jet told Amy.

"Yes, Amy agreed. Aunt Ruth needs your company." He left Amy's apartment at 1:00 a.m.

When he arrived, he noticed Ruth's car was gone. His first thoughts were that she'd had a book club or bridge club meeting and spent the night in town with her friends. He looked at her calendar on the counter and saw she'd put an 'X' on today's date. He went throughout the house calling her, then finally into the kitchen, and noticed a folded note with his name on it.

"Thank God." He sat at the kitchen table and read the note.

Jet, I am with my oldest and dearest friend. Please go to the basement and unlock the storage closet and read the letters in the boxes. The key is in the door.

Oldest and dearest friend? Who is she talking about? And at this hour? What did Aunt Ruth get herself involved in now, especially when she seems to be getting sick? She'd looked pale and wasn't very talkative the other day. His mind played tricks on him. He thought he heard a voice shouting, high and soft and from far away like a child hears calling him home.

He went to the fridge but forgot what he'd wanted when he got there. *Aunt Ruth is with her friend and she wants me to read letters.* Jet started to open the basement door, remembered it wasn't heated, reached over the sofa and took his aunt's red scarf. He went down the basement steps, walked over to the storage closet, unlocked the door and saw several small boxes, all labeled by year. When he opened the first one, he could see quite a stack of envelopes inside. Jet decided

222

it could wait till morning. *I'm going to find Aunt Ruth, probably at the hospital taking care of her friend. Why didn't she leave a telephone number?*

But before he could give up altogether, he surrendered; he felt obligated to at least read a few to please her. He took out the first box, sat on the floor, leaned against the wall and began to read the one-page letters.

In the beginning, the words seemed strange. *Your father was killed by the mob.* Letter after letter followed, detailing his mother's life, in her own words. He read about her homelessness and friends, her time at the women's shelter, and the violence against her by the mob.

While reading, he lost his vision for moments at a time. He strained tear-filled eyes, blinking over and over. Wiping his nose on his shirt sleeve, Jet hugged close the words from his mother. He had wondered about her for years, in the same silence Jenny had given to his memory.

He went through all the boxes, and finally read the last one, which told her final secret.

She had changed her name to Jenny Stone.

Jet stopped dead, sitting against that cold wall. He felt like he was feeling the aftershocks of an earthquake. He couldn't breathe; then he couldn't think. His heart was pounding like a drum.

Taking a deep, pained breath, he tried to replay her words: *His mother was Jenny Stone.* The woman he'd sent to die in the gas chamber had given birth to him and loved him.

His strong mind forced him up, forced his weak legs to move. Gripping the handrail, he stumbled up the stairs.

Abruptly, he knew where to find Aunt Ruth, and now, he had work to do. *My mother lost her son; I can bring him back.*

Jet looked at his watch. He had read over three hours, heedless of the passing time. *Dear God, it's 5:30 a.m.!*

Quickly, he called the Governor. The officer on duty at the governor's mansion told Jet the governor was on vacation. Yes, he had the number and would wake him and give him the message to call the execution hotline and ask for Jet Thomas.

Jet dashed through the house and raced to the car.

His mother's last words kept going through his mind: "The mob killed your father, and now the mob will kill your mother."

He choked back tears, took a curve too fast, hit some bushes and dirt, but managed to stay in control. "Go! Go! Go! Don't stop for anything! Please, God, *stop the clock!*" he prayed aloud.

+++

At precisely 5 a.m., two guards knocked on the cell door. Ruth and Jenny jumped. Ruth feared things were moving too quickly. Jet would surely come—wouldn't he? He had! --and she didn't care how mad Jenny would be. *I'll handle that when the time comes.*

They slowly walked out of the cell. Jenny looked at Jacob. Neither said a word.

One of the guards said, "Miss Ruth, you can only go as far as the car with Miss Stone." Ruth nodded.

As the car drove away, she kept her emotions in check, to avoid attracting attention.

Her heart heavy with despair, Ruth got into her car, praying Jet had read the letters and hurried to the prison. She drove to his office; there was no car in his parking space. *Please, God, don't let him be too late.*

+++

Jenny sat in the car, looking at a queer, seething light between night and daybreak when you cannot look long at anything before it begins to disappear. Her beautiful face focused ahead, while terror raged inside her body. Her world was destroyed. She twisted her long, nervous, manicured fingers in agony.

"Dear God," she whispered silently, "let my son know real, unconditional love from his wife, and may he give unconditional love to her and their children."

Stop it! Stop it! I want to run, get away. Don't take my life!

She closed her eyes, trying to find, in these last moments, some level of acceptance of what was coming. *Dear Lord, watch over Jet and Ruth. Please forgive me for what I've done, and what for I've failed to do.* Earlier, she'd given a note to Ruth, which contained her last wishes for Jet. Jenny knew he would do as she requested.

After a short drive, they arrived at the prison building that housed the gas chamber. Dazed and confused, Jenny walked down the hall slowly, not meeting anyone's gaze. Several times, she stumbled, and the guards caught her and put her back on her feet, to walk down that tunnel of death.

Ruth needs to bring my brush. I want to touch up my hair. We all have big plans tonight. Some semblance of calm was slowly returning.

I know that in the deepest part of Tony's heart, he blamed me for Sam and Baxter's deaths. For this, I am sorry. But I didn't deserve to be framed, just to save his life.

She looked through the open door leading into the chamber room, where the central feature was a huge black chair with heavy straps for the arms and legs. Soon, she'd be sitting in that. She shivered at the thought.

The guards turned Jenny around to face the warden. He read the death sentence to her, never looking directly into her eyes. Slowly, she turned and faced the chair again, and the guards removed her shoes. Jenny squeezed her eyes shut and almost fainted.

One of the guards whispered, "Miss Stone, if you take deep breaths, it will be over faster. Try not to fight it. When you hear the bag of pellets drop, count and take deep breaths."

With a saddened, woeful spirit, Jenny asked, "Has the governor called? My lawyer is talking with him."

"No, ma'am, but the phone is right here."

She sat in the chair. They secured her hands and feet. She looked at the observation room behind heavy glass, where several reporters were sitting with their notebooks. No cameras were permitted in the chamber. She stared down at a deep, black hole in the floor. When she raised her head, Jet was there, wearing a red scarf. The sight sent her mind spiraling. *Good, Jet will know if this is a strong chair. Will the chair keep me from falling? I can't see the bottom. Jet, don't talk to strangers. You remembered to wear red, my darling son. I love you, Jet.*

The door closed, and she was alone.

I hear the turning of a wheel and hiss of flowing liquid, the cyanide pellets dropping into the bucket of sulfuric acid, just the way the guard told me. My execution has begun. She felt an unbearable burning sensation in her mouth and nose and started coughing.

My chest is being crushed. The straps are too tight. I will take little breaths. Help me! Now, I lay me down to sleep. I hear bells ringing.

She breathed deeply, as she'd been told, and in a few minutes went limp. Foam trickled from her mouth.

+++

Outside the chamber, a phone rang.

An officer ran over to Jet. "Sir," he said quickly, "the governor is on the phone."

The doctor was listening to her heart and motioned to the observers with a nod of his head. The guard closed the curtain. Jenny Stone was pronounced dead at 6:10 a.m.

"Sir?" the officer urged. "I said, the governor is on the phone."

"Never mind," Jet said, his emotions conflicted with his decisions. "Where are they taking the body?"

"The prison always uses the Parker Funeral Home. We have a contract with them."

Jet turned and walked out of the observation room. Several photographers outside snapped his picture.

Jet left the prison and drove a short distance, until nausea and anger overwhelmed him, and he pulled off the road and stopped. A hearse passed, followed by a police car. Jet watched as the hearse approached the intersection and made a left turn. A shadow of loneliness darkened his world.

Jeremiah Elijah Thomas wept for the loss of his mother, the woman who gave life to him and for him.

How could this happen? I could have saved her. The face at the window and the touch of her hand, the beautiful woman in red desired love and respect. I hate whoever is responsible for the waste of this life.

Jet drove to the jail and went downstairs. "Jacob, are you awake?"

"Yes sir, I'm awake," Jacob said. He sat in Jenny's cell with the door open.

Jet and Jacob looked at each other. Jet sat in the chair, Jacob on the cot.

"Is she gone?" Jacob asked.

"Yes. That's why I'm here. What did you know about my mother? I know she talked to you. Why did she want to die, Jacob?" Jet demanded, his voice growing louder and hoarser. "Tell me, Jacob, so I can understand."

"So, you read her letters. Then, you know only a little part of her life," Jacob stuttered, choking on his words. "Mr. Jet, I need to read my Bible now. You're in shock and a lot of pain. Go home and talk to your mother's best friend, the person who committed herself to your mother's wishes." Jacob struggled to his feet and shuffled to his cot under the stairwell.

Jet walked to his car. While he told himself, he was not at fault, he could not help the nagging feeling that somehow, he might have discovered another solution.

His throat hurt from crying and begging God not to sacrifice his mother. Jet knew if or when he had the power, the gas chamber would never be the only execution option for the death penalty.

Around 8 a.m., he drove home and parked his car beside Ruth's old Buick. He hadn't slept for twenty-four hours; he was exhausted.

He was impatient, too. He knew the arrest of Tony Salvadore was a matter of time and urgency.

Ruth noticed Jet's pale color and his look of despair, but she couldn't bring herself to ask the question. Finally, he said, "The Governor called too late. I accomplished nothing."

Hearing those heavy words, Ruth's world turned upside down. *Now, I have the task of putting all the pieces of Jet's life together for him. For the love of my life, I will fulfil every duty, thinking of you.*

Jet reached over and they held each other. Ruth murmured words of comfort.

+++

Ruth looked at the mantle clock. Time was passing quickly. She stood and wiped her tears, looking for the strength to speak.

"Jet, I need to give you several requests from Jenny--your mother. I can say 'your mother' to you, but you must never repeat it."

She gave him a sheet of paper.

He read: *Dear Son, these are my final wishes.* When he finished reading, he concluded that his mother had decided to right a mistake even after her death. *And this* will *be done, so help me God.*

"Well?" Aunt Ruth asked.

"They will be done," Jet answered.

"Then drink some coffee and get on with it, quickly." He had to move fast to fulfil his responsibilities, so Jet refused coffee and left the house. They would already be preparing the embalming for the quiet burial at 10 a.m. in the pauper's field— lonely, unmarked graves, for the poor.

At five minutes past ten, Jet sat in his office reading the front page of the <u>Courier Times's</u> headline: *The Siren Was No Match for the Jet.* The photo showed him leaving the prison, wearing the red scarf.

If they only knew.

Jet's only solace lay in his vow that his mother's life would have meaning, would stand for something. *And for the rest of my life, I'll remember the last time we were together, and the beautiful woman holding my hand.*

Jet and Ruth could not attend the burial; Jenny had insisted they not be present, for their own safety. But at 10 a.m., at Jet's request, a police car pulled up to the gravesite. The coffin was lowered into the grave. One of the officers opened the back door of the police car, and Jacob, barefoot, shackled and hands cuffed in front of him, stepped out on the soft earth.

"Now, you just watch yourself, boy," the officer said. Jacob stood as the dirt was tossed on the coffin and raised his eyes to the heavens. He sang "Amazing Grace." And as he sang, a full burst of sun came out of the cloudy sky and flooded his face in warm light.

When he finished the song, Jacob was smiling. *I told Jenny that before I died, I wanted to feel the earth under my feet and the sun in my face. How did she make this happen?*

The officers led him back to the car.

+++

After Jenny's execution, Jacob felt defeated, broken, lonely and helpless. At times, he talked to Jenny's spirit, but soon, that hurt too much.

Meanwhile, Jenny's other last requests became Jet's crusade. Her efforts would not be wasted.

Three weeks after Jenny's execution, Jet told his secretary to locate the file for Jacob Young. He'd been caught stealing a mule at age twenty. With one phone call to the governor, and the evidence in Jet's possession, Jacob Young's life would change forever.

+++

Jet requested to be alone with Jacob. The young prosecutor spoke in a soft, nurturing tone to this black man, only a few years older than himself.

"Jacob Young, the Governor of New York has issued a pardon for the crime you committed 10 years ago. You are now a free man."

As the words became clear to Jacob, he was spellbound. The weakness in his knees persuaded him to sit down for several minutes before he could believe his good fortune. *The racing thoughts of the hardships, survival and deprivation will be replaced with liberty and freedom; my life will matter.*

With Jacob sitting in the chair, gripping the armrest and Jet sitting on the edge of his desk, Jenny's last requests outlined compassion and commitment.

"Jacob, you've also been hired as the security officer at the Hampton Apartment Building. In return, I need a favor. You'll also do a little undercover work for me."

Jet stood at his desk, looking directly at Jacob, and explained the information in his mother's requests. He sensed that Jacob was not completely surprised about the mob's involvement in Jenny's life.

"I'll do my best," Jacob responded.

Jet went over and opened his office door. A young officer came in, and Jet gave the order to remove the shackles.

By coincidence, there was a commotion outside Jet's office. Without so much as a knock, Ruth entered the room, smiling.

She quickly kissed Jet and said, "Jacob and I are leaving now."

Jet put his hand on Jacob's shoulder and said, "Good luck." He placed a key in Jacob's hand.

They travelled a few miles. Then she pulled the car to the curb and stopped. "Well, here we are," she announced. "The Hampton apartments." She noticed that Jacob stared at the condemned McDaniel building across the street for a moment.

Then he followed Ruth toward the entrance.

+++

As the weeks passed, the District Attorney's office seemed like Grand Central Station, with the comings and goings of attorneys and reporters. Governor Meyner made several visits to Jet's office, offering additional officers and other personnel, if needed, for the investigation.

Without a doubt, Jet's future was being shaped by his mother's past. She had done what she felt she must. Politicians and law-abiding citizens alike were eager to end the mob violence.

Jet remembered his mother's words: *The mob killed your father and now your mother.* Make the killing stop. The power of those words remained undiminished.

+++

Late one afternoon, Jet stood outside the McDaniel Building on a grass strip, talking with Jacob. After a heavy rain and strong winds earlier in the day, the sky cleared, the sunlight appeared; signs proving something happened. A parade of policemen and FBI agents walked past, with dozens of boxes of potential evidence.

Jet and Jacob turned as they heard the loud, distinctive voice of Tony Salvadore. He looked straight at Jet and demanded, "I want to talk to my lawyer."

Jet smiled and replied, "You'll get your chance. He's in the backseat of the second police car. You might have to wait your turn."

Jet watched as mob-boss Tony Salvadore--handcuffed, unshaven, clothes wrinkled and sleep deprived—climbed into the waiting patrol car.

"Now, Jacob." Jet looked over in a brotherly manner. Jacob was three years older than Jet. "Jacob," he said again, smiling, and this time he looked down at Jacob's large bare feet. "You *have* to wear shoes on this job. We won't even mention that it's *freezing* out here."

Jacob smiled. "Jet, you know I will, but for now I just need these toes to feel something soft, not like the jail floor."

Silence followed. They knew they'd achieved a great task. The two men, a barefoot black security guard and the lead prosecutor for the state of New York, gave each other a hug of love and respect.

+++

Jet decided after several weeks, and against his Aunt Ruth's protests, to visit his mother's grave. He purchased one red rose and drove out to Pauper's Field, at the back edge of the city cemetery. He wore a long wool black coat with a red scarf. As always, his mother's letters were on his mind.

As he stood at the gravesite, reflecting on the past few months, he did not hear the large, black car coming down the dirt road several lanes over.

Slowly, the car's back window rolled down. A bull-faced mob hit man with a semi-automatic Colt pistol looked out the window and aimed his gun sights directly on Jet's back. His finger touched the trigger and looked through the sights of his killing machine. This target would be easy.

For a moment, he froze and took his finger off the trigger. Then he rubbed his eyes and repositioned the gun.

A woman dressed in black, wearing a black veil and red gloves, appeared between his target and the car. She looked directly into the pistol barrel. Her form wavered, as though from bad television reception.

He pulled the gun inside the window and hollered to the driver, "Step on it! Get the hell out of here!" The confused driver sped out of the cemetery. The car disappeared from sight.

Jet stood beside his mother's grave, heard a noise and turned in time to see the black car racing out of the cemetery. He looked around and saw nothing unusual. Kneeling, with his hand on the pauper's grave, brave enough to cry until exhausted, he placed the rose on the mound of dirt and whispered, "**I love you, Momma**."

In the beginning--the year is 1958.

Made in the USA
Columbia, SC
05 November 2020